August Schofield: The American Dream

**Published by Writers Block Publishing LLC**
**October 2018**
**First Printing**

www.writersblockpublishingllc.com

**Author E. Davis**

www.edavisllc.com

In 2006, one weekend, I had binge-watched Tyler Perry movies and plays. That night, I had a dream that Tyler Perry brought one of my books and turned it into a C.D., I was so excited that I started praising the Lord.  Then I  woke up and shook my head, laughing at my dream, understanding that it was too much Tyler Perry.  I went back to bed and dreamed that Tyler Perry was at my job talking to my manager.  The next day, I spoke with my pastor about my dream, and he said that an influential figure will help me with my writing, and my writing will take me higher than my job.  Whenever I am inspired to write, write.

It wasn't until 2008, while working on a book, I had writer's block.  I stepped away from the work and binged watch Johnny Depp movies. I enjoyed the classics, like *Edward Scissorhands, What's Eating Gilbert Grape,*  I enjoyed the heartfelt movies like *Finding Neverland*, and went on an adventure with *Fear and Loathing in Las Vegas*, as I binged watched these movies, I found myself writing and then I realized that Johnny Depp is that influential figure that will help me with my writing.

Whenever I see Johnny Depp in a coincidence type of way, like stumble on a movie while channel surfing, or see him in my news feed, I know that I need to pay attention because some kind of creative force will come, leading me to another story.

I may never meet Johnny Depp, but if I do, I just want to say thank you for being my muse.

E. Davis

# THEN

## The Muse

**I WAS AT MY** favorite bar and grill, sitting at my favorite table, sometimes my presumed office. It was far in the corner of the restaurant. I was trying to get deep in my thoughts as I worked on my next book. Usually, I would be in the office I had built in my home. The television would be on to something that I wouldn't be tempted to pay attention to, but tonight, I needed a change of scenery. I was not able to concentrate in my office. I could have walked the streets of Manhattan and shopped. Spend money that I don't have at some boutique. As I tapped my pen against the table, I thought about calling home to talk to my daughter Joy, but I didn't have the energy to engage into her animated world and endure a long-winded conversation with every other word being, "and guess what," I love her, she is the love of my life, but I really needed to write. So here I was in the lounge of my favorite bar and grill, writing, trying to write. Right now, the atmosphere was what I needed; I was in the midst of people. I watch the people in the restaurant engage in conversation, laugh among themselves.

For my dinner, I ordered a grilled chicken sandwich with provolone cheese and mushrooms with seasoned fries. I usually don't eat the fries; I take them home and give them to Joy. As I took a bite out of my sandwich, I saw Tommy Gibbs enter the lounge; *The* Tommy Gibbs. He wasn't alone. He was accompanied by two other gentlemen. I recognized one as an actor, but I didn't know the other. Tommy was a well-known actor, a three-time Academy Award-winning actor. He was a character actor. His level of acting is uncontainable. He was not to be characterized by typecasting. Tommy played all types of roles and excelled in everyone. He played the romantic lover to the action hero. If he were to be typecast, then he would be known for playing a loner. Tommy played all types of loners, from the psychotic loner to an amusing loner or quirky loner. To me, he was one of the most gifted and talented actors of my time. I was in love with this man. Not the physical love where I wanted to bear his child, but I loved him as an actor and an artist. However, the strange part of my affection is that I was not a fan. I can count on one hand how many Tommy Gibbs movies I have seen, and he has done many. If I were to watch a Tommy Gibbs movie, I would see the movie, not just him, but I know that I would not be disappointed in the movie because of his skill as an actor. My love for Tommy Gibbs is simple; he is my muse, my inspiration.

Tommy is not my reason for why I am an author. However, he is the reason why my third book has been a New York Times bestseller for three months. Tommy, as an actor, ignites me as a writer. Although nothing in my writing has anything to do with him. I just knew that while writing my third book, I was going through writer's block. To clear my head, a friend and I went to the movies; we happened to watch a movie with Tommy Gibbs. Afterward, while talking with friends about the movie, we laughed at the eccentric role that he played. Only that particular role could have been performed by Tommy Gibbs. Somehow, the level of creativity he brought to the character challenged me to dig deep and elaborate more. It was with that book, he became my muse. I dedicated that book to him.

I watched the hostess escort Tommy and his friends to the table that happened to be next to mine. I took a deep breath. I had never met Tommy Gibbs before; if my Joy were here, she would be so excited. She loved him in the movie *Black Box*. I tried not to stare at him, but I did make several glances while he and his friends looked over their menu. He looked nice. He wore a black button-up shirt and black slacks, his dark hair tousled. The waitress brought their drinks. I watched as he ordered a steak, medium rare, and a baked potato. Then he lit a cigarette and took in a long drag. I finally exhaled. I don't smoke, but I really wanted to be at that table.

"August," Chris, my waitress, startled me. "Would you like another Coke?"

"Ah, yeah, no ice," I answered.

Considering that I was a regular at the lounge. I knew the waiters and waitresses, and they knew me too. My name is August Schofield. I'm an author. So far, I have written three novels; all three are currently on the New York best-sellers' list. I was named after August Wilson, a playwright from Pittsburgh. I, too, am from Pittsburgh. Once my first book took immediate success, I packed up my journals and my Joy and moved to New York. My writing is a gift from God. I've been writing since I was eight years old. I knew that I was going to be a successful writer; however, during my quest for literary greatness, I got sidetracked by getting married to a not-so-nice man.

Seven years later, I got divorced. The one thing that helped me weather the storms during the hurricane of matrimony was Joy. She is colorful and energetic. So many emotions come forth whenever she speaks. I named her Joy because when she was born, I was filled with so much happiness; she gave me joy. Joy, my Joy, is what I refer to her; she is my soul. I love her more than life. Joy is the most beautiful girl in the world. It may be somewhat biased to say or think so, but my Joy is so amazing. I can't imagine anyone looking into her big, brown doe-like eyes and not fall in love. I cannot imagine anyone not smiling whenever she smiles at them.

Chris brought me another glass of Coke, then disappeared to attend to her other customers. I glanced at Tommy. He sipped on whatever wine he was drinking. Although my attention was on the pages of my journal, I thought how I would love to have the courage to walk to his table and say nonchalantly:

"Mr. Gibbs, I am August Schofield, and I really admire your work."

But that is the epitome of lame. I am not some star-struck fan, but I did feel like one sitting next to the table of my muse, Thomas Michael Gibbs. –The fact that I know his full name proves that I don't need to go to his table.

I looked back at Tommy; he was laughing at something funny, something that one of his friends had said.

*What's so funny,* I wondered.

Again, I focused on my journal; then, there was loud laughter, not from him but from one of his friends.

8

Tommy smiled; he has a nice smile. He finished his cigarette, taking a final drag, and then blew smoke up into the air.

*August, stop staring at that man.*

I told myself.

I got up from my table, grabbed my cell phone, and walked into the front of the bar and grill, and called Joy. She was babysat by my brother, Xavier.

"Hi, Mommy," she said.

"Hi, baby, what are you doing?"

"Watching *Dreamgirls* with Uncle X," she answered. "I'll call you back, bye!"

She hung up on me.

"Joy!"

I stood still, almost offended. What do *Dreamgirls* have that I don't have?

I called home again. Xavier answered.

"Hey, how's the writing?" he asked.

"X., you wouldn't believe who is sitting at the table next to mine,"

"Who?"

"My muse,"

"No," "Yes," I stressed.

"Baby sister," he said.

"Yes," I whispered. "And I am the big sister."

I felt the need to defend the pecking order with my brother and me. Why? Because Xavier is taller, he feels that gives him leverage to ignore the pecking order and tease his little sister.

"Did you say something to him?" Xavier asked.

"No, what am I going to say?" I asked. "I'm thirty-four years old, not thirteen, and why would he care?"

"August, you are the bestselling author right now; he just might care."

"I'm not going to say anything, but I did call to see what Joy is doing. Why is my baby watching *Dreamgirls*?"

"Sasha," Xavier answered with a chuckle.

I sighed and then hung up the phone. He was referring to Beyoncé Knowles' alter ego, Sasha Fierce. I knew Joy was enjoying the music. There was no way that I was going to win over Jimmy Early's *Stepping to the Bad Side*. From the music to the choreography, I knew that my Joy was dancing and singing along as if she were one of the Dreamettes. I returned to my table and saw that Chris had boxed up my fries, and Tommy was now enjoying his half-cooked steak.

I sat down and focused on my writing. Within a few moments, Chris returned to my table,

"August," she said.

I looked up.

"There is a table with ladies who are reading your book for their book club. They would like to meet you."

"Okay," I grinned.

I followed Chris to a round table where four women were seated. As I approached them, they smiled at me.

"Hello," I said to them.

"Ladies, meet August Schofield," Chris introduced.

The ladies began to introduce themselves.

"Denise,"

"Beth,"

"Brandi, with an I," was the introduction.

"Monica,"

"Ladies, how are you?"

Brandi, with an I, held up my book as she puffed on a cigarette. I smiled. It was my latest book, the one dedicated to Tommy. I slowly took in a deep breath and then slowly exhaled.

"We are in a book club," Beth informed. "And your book is our book of the month. Ms. Schofield, we love your work."

"August, and thank you,"

"Can you sign our books?" Denise asked, smiling.

"Of course," I answered.

As I signed the ladies' book, we talked.

"Are you ladies from around here?"

"Yes," Beth answered. "We came in here for their hot wings, and what are the odds of meeting you?"

I grinned.

"When is your next book coming out?" Monica asked.

I quickly glanced at my table, then at Tommy, and then I looked at the ladies.

"Soon,"

"Can you tell us what it is about?" Denise asked with a grin.

I chuckled, indicating that I won't. The ladies then laughed.

"Well, ladies, I have to go, but it was a pleasure meeting you," I said.

I looked towards Chris,

"Chris, their bill, on me."

The ladies cheered and laughed. I told them again that it was a pleasure meeting them and then went back to the table. As I sat down, I glanced at Tommy. He had finished his steak, and he was smoking again. I focused on my journal.

*Focus, August focus*, I said to myself. With my muse right here, I should have no problems coming up with a good story. I had a concept; I had the characters, so now, *Write August write.*

So, while Tommy Gibbs and his friends talked and laughed with each other, I wrote in my journal. I was in the world that I created since I was eight years old. This was not some form of Neverland, but it was my imaginary place. My father called, The Land of Aug. My world was a place where power existed, not the epic fantasy power, but there was mind control, manipulating agendas, and cunning strategies. My world was not diaries or memoirs, but a place that captures you. In my work, my characters dealt with issues that may not be more than everyday agendas to the average man, but to my characters, some issues were high priorities.

I wrote down ideas for about an hour. When I finally looked up, I checked my watch. I was going to call Joy again, but I was well after ten p.m., I knew that she was off in dreamland.

I was now in need of a scenery change; the dim light in the lounge was beginning to hurt my eyes, and the second-hand smoke that I inhaled probably took fifteen years off my life. But if I leave, I might miss any opportunity that I may have to talk with Tommy. Going up to him was not an option, but at least, if I think that I have a chance, then I can stay.

Then I had this epiphany. I don't need to meet Tommy Gibbs. He is my muse. He doesn't need to know that, and I don't care if he cares, and I don't care if he doesn't care. I am not a bestselling author because of him, but I am inspired to be the best because of him.

I looked at his table. I saw one of his friends was on their cell phone. He had gotten up from the table to talk on the phone. The other friend was reading over the food bill. Then Tommy looked at me. Our eyes met. He smiled at me, and my heart stopped beating. He raised his glass to me, saluting me, and then finished his wine.

E. Davis

# NOW

## 1

**I SIT STILL WAITING** for him to blink, but instead, he just stares at me. His blank stare is disturbing, not in a haunting way but disturbing, nonetheless.   Adam Peterson. I hate Adam Peterson, well, not hate in hate him.  As a matter of fact, he is a nice guy, a real nice guy, but right now, his blank stare is irritating me; I knew that I was going to get some kind of lecture. Adam is my publisher, he acts as my agent and treats me as if he is  my manager. His disturbing stare right now is because I just told him that I have writer's block, and my next book was due a month ago.

"August, what is the problem?" he asked, finally blinking, and then sipped his apple juice.

"I don't know," I answered.

"What is the block?"

"I don't know," I said. "I have no characters, no storyline. I want to write, but I have nothing to write about."

"No, no, no, no," Adam said, standing up.

He started to pace the floor.

"Okay, okay, your first book?"

"An idea, a what-if scenario," I answered.

"Book two was somewhat of an autobiographic."

"Some parts," I said, shifting my eyes, trying to be evasive.

"Okay, book three was more of a coming-of-age type story, which was your best work yet. All three books were intriguing.  Intriguing people, intriguing situations, are you no longer intrigued, August?"

"I don't know," I answered. "Adam, we can sit all day trying to figure out my block, but that would be pointless. I am looking for something that will be--"

"August." He cut me off. "I don't want to hear you, Gatsby crap!"

I sighed. *The Great Gatsby* is one of my favorite books; I would love to write a book that is that amazing.

"I know what is causing your block," Adam said, walking up to me. "You have grown comfortable, content with your new lifestyle. Life is good. Joy is happy. You need some kind of stimulation. Fire under your-,"

"No," I said, quickly cutting him off. I was afraid of where he was going to put the fire. "My life is full of intriguing and stimulating events."

"Name one,"

I sat and thought for a moment. I had no response.

"August, have you met anyone since you've been in New York?"

"Yes, I met quite a few interesting people," I answered.

"Do they inspire you?"

"They are characters, I must say,"

"August, how's your father?"

"My dad is good, and no, there are no dramatic childhood stories. My father and I are perfect."

"Boyfriends," Adams asked.

"When do I have time for a boyfriend? I just sat and watched you not blink for half an hour."

I look at my watch. It was only two o'clock. I had enough of Adam.

"Adam, I have to get Joy."
I stand up.
"August," Adam said.
I look at him.
"I need a book; soon."

I nod my head in understanding the now demand for my book. I leave. I don't have to pick Joy up until four o'clock. I just had to get away from Adam. I went to the bookstore and hid in the back. I sit down in the big, comfortable chair, pull my journal from my bag, and jot down some ideas.

What in the world am I going to write about? I have no clue. Here I am in a bookstore surrounded by many, many authors from my favorites, like Toni Morrison, F. Scott Fitzgerald, to those I have never heard of, but I can assume equally good writers. There are autobiographies, memoirs, classic literature, mystery and suspense thrillers, and epic sci-fi adventures. I get up and slowly walk around the bookstore, looking at every book. I look at the description of the book, love stories- how sweet. Suspense- how gripping. Mysteries- who did it, who killed him?

I walk to the children's section and see books that would cause Joy to spend my money. I look at the author's description of some of them. One of them said: Inspired by childhood events. Should I write a children's book? I asked myself. No, I answered myself. I am not a children's writer. Although Joy does keep me entertained in her world where she reigns as either queen, empress, or some form of madam ruler, and I am her humble servant or sidekick.

I look at the books that represent some kind of sisterhood, such as *Waiting to Exhale, The Sisterhood of Traveling Pants, The Divine Secrets of the Ya-Ya Sisterhood.* I thought about my friends, comical individuals, each with their own unique personalities. I began to wonder if my friends are some form of inspiration.

I look at my watch and see that this time it is time to get Joy from school. With the urgency of my book, I hope that she doesn't want to go anywhere in particular. I just want to go home, eat Chinese food, and hide in bed.

**AS I APPLY DUCK** sauce on my egg roll, I listen to Joy tell me about the adventures from school.

"Mommy, Amanda always bosses me around. I told her, 'You're not the boss of me,' she looked at me and said. 'I'm not, Joy.' But I know she is trying to be Mommy. She always tells me what to do."

I chuckle.

Leave it to my daughter to find a conspiracy. I was more than happy when I got Joy from school, and she didn't want to go anywhere. So, my night is Chinese food and Sponge Bob. As I listened to Joy, I thought about her conspiracy theory with her classmate. Is there a story in that? I shake my head at the concept.

~

**WITH JOY ON THE** couch in the world of Bikini Bottom. I sit at the dining table with my pen and journal and wonder what is going to stimulate me enough to write a bestseller. I look at Joy being hypnotized by Sponge Bob, and I wonder what inspired the creators of Sponge Bob to come up with their concept. A sponge, living in an ocean, and wearing pants.

*Why is it so easy for them and not me?* I asked myself.

My eyes scanned my living room. I get up from the table and walk through my home. Adam said that I have gotten comfortable. Is that true? I live in a four-bedroom brownstone in the Upper West Side of New York in Manhattan that I adore, a bit pricey, but I want the essence of a writer in New York. I want the *Sex in the City* Carrie Bradshaw, New York. I would love to live the fabulous life with my three best friends and my Mr. Big, but instead, I live a quiet and sweet life with my Joy. I spend my nights writing or watching SpongeBob. Instead of drinking Cosmopolitans, I drink decaffeinated green tea or hot cocoa. I don't have a 9-5 job that I have to beat rush hour to get to. I have a bedroom that I turned into an office to report to after I drop Joy off at school or Day Camp during the summers. I can come and go as I please. So, is Adam right? Have I gotten comfortable? I don't have Carrie Bradshaw's sense of style, but I do have a few nice black dresses in my closet for special occasions, where I can serve Audrey Hepburn glamour. I am not a multi-millionaire, but with my book sales, I am living a pretty good life. So maybe, Adam has a point; I have gotten comfortable. There is no quest for a best seller at the moment because I am spending my nights eating Chinese food and watching Sponge Bob. I walk back to the dining table, sit back down, and let out a sigh as I look at my journal.

"Mommy, look!" Joy exclaimed; she was pointing to the television.

I get up from the table and walk to the television to see what she is pointing at. There is an advertisement for Tommy Gibbs' new movie. He is playing a clown, a disturbing but amusing clown. I chuckle, my muse.

"Mommy, can we go see that?" Joy asks, smiling.

"No Joy, that movie is rated R."

Joy sighs.

My muse simulates me. Well, he did with my last book. Can he ignite my creativity? Taking in a deep breath, I close my eyes and walk back to the dining table to attempt to write. I sit at the table thinking. I literally have nothing to write about. I look in Joy's direction, and suddenly I am startled. Tommy Gibbs is sitting in the big easy chair by the window. I inhale, holding my breath. I tend to hallucinate. I usually do it whenever I am writing.

I would see images of my characters. I put myself into whatever scene my characters are in, and I would watch them interact with each other, and I would write everything down. I make sure that I mention their facial expressions, them running their fingers through their hair. Any kind of nervous quirks like biting their nails or cracking their knuckles, but Tommy Gibbs-really? Why am I seeing Tommy Gibbs? He looks real, too real, more than a hallucination. I don't know what to say or do. I never hallucinated real people, just figments of my imagination. But here in my living room is this man, or the image of this man. Is he a figment of my imagination? I don't know if I should approach him or stay in my seat. The last time I saw him in person, I was too intimidated by his persona to approach him. I heard that he was a humble and down-to-earth man. However, considering my everyday status, the last thing he needed was me disturbing his evening with my star-struck fan fair. Plus, at the time, there was no reason or need for me to meet him, but now, what is the reason that his image is in my house?

I think for a moment. If Tommy Gibbs is my muse, then he must be here to inspire me, but at the moment, I don't feel anything creatively. I look at Joy; she is still in Bikini Bottom. She doesn't notice him. I look at Tommy; he looks at me as if he is waiting for me to do something.

"Joy," I said, looking at Tommy Gibbs. "Go take your bath,"

"Awe, Mom," she whined.

"Yeah, go; you can have ice cream afterward."

"Okay," she said.

I watched Joy go upstairs. Once she was out of sight, I looked at Tommy again. He approaches me. My heart beats rapidly in my chest.

"What's wrong?" he asks.

"Did Joy see you?" I ask.

He shakes his head.

"I'm in here," he said, pointing to his head.

I am caught off guard by his coolness. He talks to me as if he knows me. I don't understand what is going on, why I am seeing this man. Clearly looking at him, he looks very real, not a hallucination. He looks at me, waiting for me to say something to him. I don't know what to say to him. He is my muse. Is he here to help me write?

"I have writer's block," I inform him.

A minute passes.

"What's your block?" he asks.

"I don't know; I just can't write," I answered, shrugging my shoulders.

"Write what you know," Tommy suggested.

"I don't know anything," I said.

I walk to the couch and sit down.

"What do you mean, you don't know anything?" Tommy asks, following me.

He sits next to me. He smells good. I am hallucinating the scent of this man; I need help. As odd as this situation is, I am strangely comfortable with him. I look into his eyes. He has trusting eyes. I grin, accepting this image. I slowly inhaled and then turned away from him.

"Write a love story," he suggested.

"Done," I said. "I even wrote a type of lover's lament."

"Any of these stories about you?" Tommy asks.

"There are hints of real events," I answered, trying my best to be vague. "But I am a what- ifer,"

"A what- ifer?"

Tommy sits and thinks for a moment,

"What if," he asked.

I nodded.

"Well, most stories are what-ifs, but the real element is to have some kind of idea that is unexpected. Don't let them see it coming."

"I know," I said. "I know, but I am stuck. I am blocked. I have literature constipation. It is so easy for the other writers. Terry McMillan, hmmm, what if a middle-aged woman gets her groove back? And now she is writing sequels to her best sellers. John Grisham, what if an underdog lawyer took a legal case raining havoc on the whole world? What if a Sponge named Bob lives at the bottom of the sea wearing square pants!" I jumped up from the couch.

"August, okay," Tommy said.

I sat back down. I grab the remote control to turn the channel. For some reason, I turned on a music channel, and a Guns-N-Roses song, *November Rain,* was playing.

"This is a good song," Tommy said.

"It's a sad song," I said softly. "What do you think it means?"

"A romance that just ran its course," Tommy answered. "What if,"

"No, that happens," I answered.

Joy comes back down the steps, hopping on each step as she comes down. When she finally gets to the bottom of the steps, she smiles at me. Tommy is gone.

"What happened to Sponge Bob?"

I turned the channel back to Sponge Bob and then went to get ice cream.


Joy wakes up early to fix breakfast and to endure another Sponge Bob marathon.

"Mommy has to write," I said.

"Okay, can I have an egg sandwich with lots of cheese?"

"Sure," I said.

Joy scurries away to watch her marathon. I fixed her an egg sandwich, which is an omelet with extra cheese on wheat bread. I see that Joy is content; I attempt to write. I have my journal and my laptop handy. I sit at the dining table and get myself mentally prepared; the song *November Rain* is playing in my head. I shook my head, trying to get rid of the song. I think about things that I would like to write; as I look through the pages in my journal and try to ponder some of the ideas I had jotted down, I hear Axl Rose singing. I sighed.

*Don't fight it;* I heard a voice whisper.

Not paying too much attention to the voice, I continued to try to write and try to look at my ideas. I look up from my work to make sure Joy is good. She is no longer in my living room but in Bikini Bottom. I shake my head at the concept. I focus back on my work, and then I hear the song again. Again, I shake my head.

*Let it play;* I hear a voice to say.
I looked around to see who was speaking.
*Think about it.* The voice says again.
*Think about it?* I asked myself. *Think about what?*
No response. I take a deep breath and look through my notes again. As I write a few things down, I start swaying with the melody of *November Rain*. I tilt my head back and sigh.
*Why is this song in my head?* I ask myself. I don't like heavy metal. I don't listen to heavy metal.

The only time I really listened to *November Rain* was when the song first came out, and that was back in 1992 for me; that was sixteen years ago. I never really gave much thought to the song except for Slash's guitar solo at the end. However, for some strange reason, the song plays in my head loudly as if I am actually listening to it on the radio.

*Take it in,* - repeated the voice.

*Who is that?* I ask.

"Joy, what are you talking about?" I ask her.

For that moment, she leaves Bikini Bottom and looks up at me. Her moon-shaped eyes question my outburst. I can tell that she doesn't know what I am talking about. I shake my head, indicating to her, never mind.

"Sorry, baby," I murmured.

I let out a sigh.

*Think,* said the voice.

*Think* about what? I ask.

I get up from my seat and look around. I feel like a madwoman on a search for something. I look under the table. I look in the kitchen. I look behind my curtains. There is nothing and no one here but Joy and me. I go back to the table and sit down.

"I am crazy. I am actually a crazy person." I state, referring to myself.

There is no one here. Just me and Joy, and then, like nails on a chalkboard, I hear that Sponge Bob's annoying laugh and then Joy's sweet, adorable little girl laugh. I want to crawl into bed and go to sleep forever. I feel weird because *November Rain* still echoes in my head.

I realize that I am not going to get past this song. I need to listen to it for me to move on from it.

I go to YouTube and pull up *November Rain* on my laptop, put my earbuds in, and listen to Axel Rose croon.

*When I look into your eyes*
*I can see a love restraint*
*But darling, when I hold you*
*Don't you know I feel the same?*

The word that sticks out is restraint. Restrain, reserved; to hold back; they're holding back: Axel sees a love restrained. But Axel said that whenever he holds her, he is holding back too.

*Cause nothing lasts forever,*
*And we both know hearts can change.*

Changed hearts? I close my eyes and begin to see two people, a man and a woman, not young but not old. For some reason, they had fallen out of love. Why would they fall out of love? Have their lives become routine, where nothing is exciting?

*Love is your stimulation*, said that voice.
I don't reply; just continue to listen.

*And it's hard to hold a candle in the cold*
*November rain.*

*August*, I heard my name.

This time, the voice was familiar. I shift my eyes to where I hear the voice from. I see no one. I put my head in my hands and sigh.

*August,* repeated the voice.

I sit up, and sitting in front of me is Tommy Gibbs. I take a deep breath. Again, like last night, he is in plain sight. Joy could see him if she were ever to leave Bikini Bottom and visit her mother in Manhattan.

He looks at me with a grin as if I am supposed to know why he is sitting in front of me, but he seemed somewhat amused because I could not understand why he was in front of me. I look at my surroundings, my journal, and my Joy.

*You're okay, she can't see me. I'm in here.*

Tommy Gibbs points to his head.

*You're here to help me write,* I ask.

He nods.

*What am I going to write about? I have writer's block.*

*What's on your mind, August?*

*For starters, this crazy song is in my head.* I complained.

Tommy knowingly nods his head. I look at him.

*You know this?*

He doesn't respond. At that moment, I realized that there is something in *November Rain* that I had to write about.

*Tommy, I don't know anything about this song.*

*Listen to it,* he merely said.

I turn my music back on and listen to Axel.

*If we can take the time to lay it on the line*
*I could rest my head just knowing that*
*You are mine. So if you want to love me*
*Then, darling, don't refrain*
*Or I'll just end up walking in the cold*
*November Rain.*

Refrain, there goes that word again. I have to think,

Who's refraining, I ask myself.

I close my eyes and begin to feel the music. I set the scene. I see the two: a man, he is handsome and tall. He stands about six feet. He is in his sixties and good-looking, distinguished. His wife, a beautiful woman, is not yet sixty. She has a quiet, classic beauty. Every time her husband looks at her, he smiles. But whenever she looks at him, she smiles with her mouth, but her eyes- her eyes say something different.

*Oh my, what's missing?* I ask myself. *She is the one who is restraining. What is she refraining from?*

Each kiss he gives her says, "I love you."

She smiles and looks away what appearing to be bashful. She's not bashful, just holding back. She doesn't want to get too close; she doesn't want to get too intimate.

*Why is she holding back?*

He knows her; he sees the distance but chooses not to confront it. He smiles, hiding his concern. To avoid intimacy or any tender moment, she breaks from his embrace to run errands or do whatever chore.

*What's wrong? I asked.*
I looked up at Tommy.
*What's the matter? I ask.*
Axel continues to croons.

*I know that you can love me*
*When there's no one left to blame*
*So never mind the darkness*
*We can still find the way.*


*How did they lose their way in the first place? I* asked.

I see them. I see their history.

She is attentive, the perfect wife. She pays attention to detail. She hemmed the slacks and sewed on the buttons. She had made a perfect and peaceful home. She never caused embarrassment to her family or to his family. Never argumentative, always pleasing, and sex was never an issue. She is always willing and available for lovemaking not out of wifely duty but for pure pleasure, physical and not emotional. He needed to feel her in his heart. He loved her more than anything.

He almost lost her not once but twice. Once upon a time, he was fickle and self-centered. He promised her commitment, but when it was time to fully commit, he broke her heart. Then one day, he woke up and realized that she was the one good thing in his life, and he was not going to live another day without her.

He looked for her and found her; he promised to never break her heart again. He wined her and dined her.

He knew that he had to work hard to gain her trust back. He knew that it would be a long haul, but no matter how long it took, he was going to work for her trust, for her heart.

"I will walk through fires for you," he proclaimed his love.

Whenever he felt the distance between them. He looks her in the eyes and says:

"I love you," he said.

She grins a sweet grin, receiving his words. She responds with a passionate kiss.

"Do you love me?" he would ask.

"What do you think?" she would say, looking at him with tender eyes that allowed him to think that she loved him.

She managed to change the subject by talking about the children or what new with the neighbors.

He believed that she loved him. She wouldn't be here if she didn't love him, but at times her evasive demeanor still troubled him. He looked at her and wondered if he was just paranoid or insecure. And he would often hope that one day she would be moved with passion and express that she loved him, but in thirty years of marriage, she would never verbally communicate that she loved him. Her actions would say that she loves him, but the distance would say.

"I'm not ready to trust you,"

*Why won't she just let go?* I asked Tommy.

Tommy doesn't respond, but Axel does.

*We've been through this such a long, long time*
*Just trying to kill the pain.*

Then one day, he finds something. The evidence that he needs to know for sure that she has never forgiven him- that she never fully trusted him.

"It's just for a just in case situation," she explains evasively.

"Just in case of what?" he interrogated.

"Emergencies," she answers quickly.

This is more than just a rainy-day fund. There will always be something for the children in case of emergencies. Money never had an issue. Both had good-paying jobs, stocks in various companies, insurance on everything. There is a definitely secure safety net.

"What are you doing?" he asked, not satisfied by her response.

"I just want to make sure that I'm okay if something happens?"

"What's something?" he asked.

She doesn't answer. He realizes that after all these years, she still thinks he is going to leave. That he is going to break his promise.

"How long am I going to pay for the past?" he asks her coolly.

"I just want to make sure that I'm okay."

"You're more than okay," he said. "Right here,"

"Yes, but I don't want to-," she stops talking.

"Don't want to what?" he interrogates.

He looks at her with intense eyes piercing into her. She wants to break away and go hide, but his intense stare is holding her in place. His eyes look at the evidence, and it is clear that if anything happens, she had a Plan B.

"You don't want to rely on me. If you rely on me, then it means you have to trust me. You don't want to trust me because if you trust me, then it means that you have to forgive me."

"I do forgive you," she defends herself.

"Do you?" he asked with much doubt.

"Yes," she said in defense.

"Do you love me?" he asked.

She looked away. She will not relinquish control.

"After thirty years, you still can't tell me that you love me," He says, feeling defeated.

"My actions should tell you. I am good to you."

*Is she for real?* I ask.

"I need to hear it," he said.

His heart was breaking.

"It's nice to be told." He said softly.

"You know how I feel," she commented.

Tears were in his eyes, his throat tightened up. He wants to cry. Thirty years and he will forever pay for his actions for hurting her when they were young.

"Haven't I lived up to my word that I would never hurt you again?" He asked.

As tears fell from her eyes, she nods her head.

"Then tell me what more do you need," he requests, feeling hopeless.

Rapidly I typed away on my laptop. I wrote about the perfect yet turbulent marriage of these two characters. They had two children: a boy and a girl.

*Tommy, I said, Children are involved?*

My heart breaks. Considering that I am a divorced mother, separation can be devastating to a child. However, in my defense, it was the best thing for Joy. Unfortunately, my Joy saw the pain that I was in; it broke my heart that she is so young and knows so much. I know that at times she wonders if her father will come around to see her without causing me pain. In my story, did the children sense the emotional strain on their parents' relationship? I shake my head as I continue to develop my story. The children did not know of the emotional strain, because their mother went undetected because their mother made a pleasant home. They never saw their parents argue. Mom made sure that every Father's Day, there was a wonderful dinner, and for his birthday, he was thankful for another wonderful year with his family. In their eyes, when they saw their mother smile at their father. Her smile was a genuine smile; nothing forced. They also watch their father pour all his energy into seeing their mother happy. He lavished her in diamonds and pearls. The daughter measures men to the values of her father. She asked her mother what made her so sure that Dad was the one.

"How did you know that Daddy was the one?"

She wasn't sure how to answer that question, considering the lack of trust that she still harbored inside her heart. She had to think of the years of their marriage. He was thoughtful, faithful, attentive, and giving.

"He's a good provider," was her response.

"Daddy said that he couldn't imagine life without you," the daughter said with a smile.

She smiles at her daughter,

"Your father is a good man, and whatever man you chose will be just as good as him."

*Let it go, I said.* It's been thirty years.

I never experienced such creativity. I am able to literally see my character in front of me. I know that I am at home with my daughter writing. I can look at my things, such as my dining room table, my living room furniture, but I am in another world. In the world of these characters, this man and this woman. I am witnessing them as they interact with each other. I am literally in the center of this story, my story. I look at Tommy; he nods his head, indicating for me to continue. I walk towards her, the mother, the wife. I can look into her eyes. She has soft, lovely eyes. They are tender. Whenever the subject on expounding on the love she has for her husband, her eyes spoke of pain and loneliness, and her demeanor suddenly changed; she became aloof.

I look at Tommy; *What do I do?* I ask.

*Don't let them see it coming,* he answered.

I wrote for hours.  Like a zombie, I managed to fix Joy's lunch and dinner, and by nine o'clock, I tucked her in bed, and she went to sleep, and I continued to write.

## "AUGUST!" HE SHOUTS.

I jumped, startled.  I look at my surroundings.  I am on the couch, and my brother Xavier is staring at me as if I'm something strange.  Joy is behind him eating a dry bowl of cereal, Captain Crunch Peanut Butter Crunch.

"X.?" I ask, sitting up. "What's going on?"

"You tell me, girl, I've been calling and calling.  I came over to see if you wanted to get some breakfast, and you got the phone turned off."

X's eyes scan my living room.  He sees my laptop and journal.

"Writing," he said. "You're in the Land of Aug, and the baby is over here eating dry cereal."

"X, she likes it like that."

"No, she doesn't," he says, looking at Joy.

She smiles at him with a mouth full of peanut butter balls.

I sit back on the couch, trying to remember what had happened.  The last thing I remember was when I was at the table writing.  I looked around to see if Tommy is here, but he is gone. Did I write myself to sleep?

"I tell you what," X. fussed, "this book better be a best seller for you to be zoned out!"

My brother is in his fussing mood. He bosses me around, and I'm the big sister.  I pay him no attention.  I am too focused on my book to pay any attention to him.  I walk to the table with my laptop and journal.

"Get dress, Sweet," my brother said to Joy. "Uncle is taking you out for breakfast."

My brother glares his eyes at me.

"No one hears from you, sees you."

"X. hush, our family doesn't live here."

"I know that our family don't live here. But what is the matter with you where you can't call folks? Don't get money and start acting funny. "

Whenever my little brother gets into one of his moods, he fusses and makes no sense. Ever since my first book was published and I had a few extra dollars, I moved my brother to New York with me, just my brother. Once X got settled in New York, he opened up a small bookstore where he proudly displays my books in the front window.

"And what in the world are you listening to over here!"

*November Rain* is playing on my stereo. I watch as X walks to my stereo and turns it off. I must have burned a copy of *November Rain* and played it repetitively. As my brother fusses, I look at my notes, and to my surprise, my book is finished.

*This book is finished?* I ask myself.

My document is saved on my laptop.

I finished this?

I have never started and finished a book in a night before. I look back at my X. He is still fussing and too busy to notice how confused I am.

"X, I started writing this book yesterday, and now it's morning."

"Surprising how the life is in the Land of Aug," He says sarcastically.

"Come on, let's get something to eat."

"X, just take Joy out. I have -,"

"August, give me an hour?"

"Okay,"

Joy and I quickly went upstairs to shower and then off to breakfast.

**AS WE EAT BREAKFAST,** my brother talks about everything under the sun, from politics to religion. With him, everything is a conspiracy. This is where Joy gets it from. I try to listen, but I keep zoning in and out of the conversation. I am still marveling at the fact that I finished my book in one day. Will the public like it? Tommy said to me not to let them see it coming and did that, I think. The outcome is not what is to be expected. Right at this moment, I wanted to be at home, reading, getting back into the lives of my characters.

"Mommy!" Joy startles me.

"What?"

"I gotta go to the bathroom," she said.

I sigh,

"Oh,"

"August, where you at?" X asks.

"Xavier, don't start,"

I take Joy to the bathroom. When we returned to the table, my brother waits with dessert, a large cookie for Joy, and an apple pie for him and me. He looks at me.

"August," my brother said. "Your writing has you this stressed out?"

"I'm on a deadline, and I have writer's block. I started brainstorming yesterday morning. I mean really having some good ideas and writing, and it's finished. I mean, I finished it in one day. I have never finished a book that fast."

"Must be a good book," X. said.

I smile.

"August, you're known to go off in Land of Aug-,"

"Xavier, don't put me in the Land of Aug," I said quickly. "I was right there, right in the center."

"Relax, August, I'm just saying when you write, you zone out, and you don't come back until your work is done. I am proud of you, August; you know that my big sister is a famous artist. But the zoning out makes me nervous."

"Why,"

"Because you're a mother,"

"Excuse me,"

"Eating dry cereal is not fine for a kid. For a snack, yeah, but not when they're waiting for their parents to wake up."

I could not believe that my little brother is making me seem as if I was an unfit mother. He has no children. My brother wants to be the ultimate bachelor.

"How many kids do you have?" I snap.

X. holds his hands up, surrendering to me.

"Okay, okay, I'm being judgmental. I'm just saying, you have been through a lot, you are in a new realm, and I want to make sure you're good."

I inhale and exhale. My brother means well. He and I are five years apart, me being older. However, ever since he or I can remember, he has always treated me as if he is the older brother and I am his kid sister. From the moment X. could speak, it was,

"Aug, get this. Aug do that."

Being the perfect big sister, I did this, I got that. Now, I sit across from my brother as my daughter sits beside him eating this giant cookie, my kid brother condemning me because Joy likes to eat dry cereal, and I was writing. I want to punch him and show him who the boss really is. I am under a lot of stress. Trying to understand how I hallucinated Tommy Gibbs, how I wrote a book in a day, and trying to obtain the ultimate goal; to write my Gatsby.

"Maybe, if you know that you are going to get busy, hire an assistant. You are established enough to do that."

"I'm not hiring an assistant; I have too much to do," I say.

**I SIT IN ADAM'S OFFICE;** instead of his non-blinking stare, he stares at me with a wide grin making him look like Jack Nicholson's Joker.

"You had writer's block," he said, then laughed. "Writers' block, Oh August! You are a genius, baby!"

I watch as he rambles on.

"August baby, this book is wonderful; it's your best work yet! This book is your *Great Gatsby!* When did you start writing this?"

"Last Saturday," I answered.

"I got the email, Sunday. You write this in a day?" He asks.

He looks at me, still with the Joker's grin, but he looks like one of the Joker's victims, whose smile is frozen.

"Tell me that you did not plagiarize because I will kill you. I will shoot you in the head right now."

"No," I said "Adam,"

The Joker smile is now gone, and that non-blinking disturbing-like stare is back. It amazes me how calm he is when he is threatening to take my life.

"No, Adam, I just-," I sigh.

"Just what, girl, talk to me."

"Calm down and blink!" I snap.

I waited a minute. I take a deep breath.

"It was such a surreal experience; I was right there in the midst of my work. I could see, feel and smell everything."

As I explain the situation to him, he smiles, like a normal person. I want to hit him hard.

"August, my love," he said to me.

My love, I scoff. Just five minutes prior, he was going kill me; now I was his love. I hate him.

"This is going to be a masterpiece. You know why? Because it is going to make every seasoned middle-aged couple question their love for each other. Think, now that the kids are grown and gone, do they continue on together pulling from their love, that love that sealed them in from the beginning? Or do they look at each other and realize that it's over?"

"Adam, my book is not to break up the old couples." I protest.

I watch Adam walk around his desk to his seat. He sits down and begins to type rapidly on the computer.

"Per Google," he continued. "the definition of the American Dream is, 'the national ethos of the United States, the set of ideals, (Democracy Rights, Liberty, Opportunity, and Equality) in which freedom includes the opportunity for prosperity and success, and an upward social mobility for the family and children, achiever through hard work in a society with few...,'."

He peeks from around his computer and looks at me with his wide non-blinking eyes. I wish I had a dart gun because I would shoot him.

"Listen, they, your characters, have lived the dream. He wanted her, he got her, they get married, had kids, and lived the good life. He realized he had no life without her, so he went and got her. Very Jay Gatsby in Tom Buchanon's face. They lived a prosperous life, and when he thinks that they are at the pinnacle of the dream- it is snatched from under him! Gatsby! He thinks Daisy is on the way, and he is shot in the back."

Now I am looking at him, not blinking.

"Get ready for an explosive book tour," Adam said.

"I can't do a book tour; I have Joy-,"

I begin as Adam comes from around his desk.

"Get a nanny,"

"A nanny! No one watches my kid, but X.

"Tell him to watch the kid," Adam said, very coolly.

"How long with this book tour last?"

"As long as I say,"

Immediately, I think of Adam as Ike Turner, and I am Tina, and I better get on that stage. I sighed.

"Relax, August, you're not going on a world tour, a month. You can hit up a few major cities, L.A, Houston, maybe got back to Pittsburgh. It will be perfect. I'll notify your publicist.

I stand up, offering no response because I know it's not going to matter.

"I gotta run, talk to you later."

Adam stands up and reaches his arms out to me,

"Love me, baby," he says.

I glared at him but still leaned in and hugged him. He kisses me on my cheek, he is so..., I hate him.

**I SIT IN X'S BOOKSTORE** sipping on a free hazelnut latte. I told him about the upcoming book tour and expressed my doubts. I have never done a book tour before. I did the books signings in the local bookstores, and my brother has me doing a signing at his bookstore.

"August, this is a good opportunity," X. said.

"What about Joy,"

"I will keep her," X volunteered.

"What's this?" I ask with sarcasm. "One minute you are calling me unfit and the next minute-,"

"No, you let your writing distract you from her where she is left to fend for herself. In this case, you are working."

If my brother only knew that she actually likes to eat dry Captin Crunch Peanut Butter Puffs.

"August, when you know that you're going to get busy, hire an assistant. When will the tour start?"

"He is looking towards June,"

"Perfect," X said. "I can take Sweet to Pittsburgh to visit her family."

"What about your bookstore?" I asked. "You're going to just shut down?"

"No, I have an assistant; understand."

I sip my latte.

## 2

**I SIT IN THE SPARE** room in my home that I turned into my office looking over my manuscript.

As confused as I am that I wrote the book in a day, I am longing for that escape. Right now, Joy is at school, and I can take some time to escape, but I am hesitant. What if I get too caught up that I forget to get Joy from school? So instead of escaping and dealing with the wrath of Xavier Maurice Schofield, I decided to sit in the quiet of my office reading my manuscript.

I should appreciate the silence. No sounds are coming from Bikini Bottom. I don't hear Axel crooning. Just the sounds of the clock ticking on the wall. I wanted to escape again into the world of my characters, or I am teased, the Land of Aug. Writing is a great escape for me. Ever since I was a little girl, my gift of imagination allowed me to go anywhere I wanted to go. Be whoever I wanted to be, lived how I wanted to live. I have gotten so caught up in the lives of my characters that they can interact with my daily life. Even though I am the author, I have no control over my characters. I have to allow them their independence, to make their own decision.

For example, once, I had a parent-teacher conference with one of Joy's teachers. As I was listening to her go over the work done in class, I looked toward the window and saw one of my characters. She was sitting by the window looking outside. At the time, I was writing about a particular situation, and this character had a decision to make.

I looked back at Joy's teacher, I smiled and nodded, indicating that I was paying attention, but all I heard coming from her was Charlie's Brown's,

"Wah, wah, wah, wah, wah," –American translation, "Joy is a pleasure to have,"

"Thank you," I said.

The Land of Aug, as my family puts it, puts me in a type of tranquility in La-La Land. No matter the situations that my characters may have to deal with, turmoil or pleasure, when I write, there is solace. Just like my current book, as crazy as the character's situation was, the writing brought a type of escape for me.

"You can't hide from the world, August." My father used to say.

"I'm not hiding," I said. "I'm..," the words would never come to me when I tried to explain my reasons for wanting to escape.

My father would chuckle.

"Go away for a while,"

WE DECIDED TO MEET at a local coffee shop. From the moment I saw her, I was impressed. A petite brown beauty with a conservative style; pearl necklace with pearl stud earrings. Her hairstyle is a bob-like hairstyle. She wears a light pink cardigan over a soft yellow shirt, and a pair of boot cut khaki pants, brown high heeled Mary Jane shoes. There is a thin gold ring on the middle finger of her right hand with peach color rhinestones. As she talks to me, I looked over her resume, which was very impressive. She worked as a paralegal for a major law firm in New York. After much nagging and pestering, my kid brother convinced me to hire an assistant. Her name is Maya Cook. Maya was quick to tell me that she was named after Maya Angelou, and she found it ironic that she was being interviewed by me, a writer, who is named after August Wilson.

"My mom is a big fan," she tells me, smiling.

As adorable as she is, her smile is too much. She smiles at me as if she is meeting some kind of royal. I grin and look over her resume again. It is too impressive.

"Thank you," I said, smiling. "Your resume is impressive, too impressive. Why become a personal assistant to a writer when you could have had your law degree?"

"The law firm that I worked for went under too many rainmakers." She says.

Although her face was soft and pretty, that wide overzealous smile is gone.

I nodded my head, understanding. I look over her resume again. From what I see, she seems reliable and responsible, but my concern is what I would really need an assistant for. I see X's eyes looking at me. I inhale and then exhale.

"All I would need you to do is handle the small insignificant matters whenever I need to write."

Maya nods her head.

"Can you start today?"

"Yes," she said, smiling.

"Okay," I responded, looking at my watch.

It is time to get Joy from school.

"I have to run; I have to get my daughter. I am going to email you my publisher's information, and he will let you know about the upcoming book tour. Will you be able to come with me?"

"Travel with August Schofield?" Maya asks, smiling.

She is smiling that over-the-top smile again. I blush.

"You're acting as if I am famous," I am standing up.

"You are the black Carrie Bradshaw," she says.

I can't help but smile at that comment until I look down at my clothes and see nothing Carrie Bradshaw; I wear a pair of dark denim Capri jeans, black Mary Jane heels, and a black T-Shirt from Old Navy. My hair is pulled up and pinned into a bun, and I wear modest jewelry, small black diamond stud earrings. Maya laughs at my observation of my clothing to her comparison. She stands up.

"Just because you are not wearing a pair of Manolo's doesn't make you less Carrie,"

She grins.

"Um, okay, talk with you later," I said.

JOY AND I WALK through the park. It is a lovely, warm spring day. With Joy going away with X, I want to spend as much time with her as possible. She and I have never been apart. I hold her hand, she walks along happily, talking about her day.

"Are you excited about going away with X?"

"Yes!" she said quickly. "X said that he was going to take me to Kennywood, the Pixburgh Zoo,"

"Pittsburg Zoo," I corrected.

"That's what I said, Mommy, Pixburgh." Joy said, looking up at me.

Her doe eyes cause my heart to skip a beat. She smiles at me, and like gravity, her smiles pull my emotions in, and I laugh back at her; I love my baby.

Joy looks around the park and sees a man with a cart that is selling Italian Ice.

"Mommy, can I have Italian Ice?" Joy asked.

Handing Joy a dollar bill, she quickly races off to the cart that is selling Italian ice. The spring season released a cool but comforting breeze. The day is a simply beautiful, clear sky, bright, the warm sun smiling down upon us. The leaves and flowers are now in full bloom, ready for the start of the summer. Joy runs back to me with her cherry Italian ice. She sits down on the bench, her legs swinging as she enjoys her treat.

"You going to miss me when you're gone?" I ask.

"Hmm," she said, placing the spoon of red slush in her mouth.

She closes her eyes, savoring the sugar.

"Don't eat that too fast,"

Joy nods her head, shoving another spoonful in her mouth.

"Mommy," she said with exaggeration. "Uncle X. said that I'm going to meet family."

"Yeah, you have some relatives that you haven't met yet, cousins, aunts, and uncles. That would be nice, huh?"

Joy doesn't reply to me; she continues to eat.

I let out a sigh. She is growing up so fast, too fast. It was just yesterday that she was my chunky little girl baby that loved to smile. My Joy would cuddle next to me, laying her chubby face next to mine, and just giggle. Then Joy would wrap her arms around my neck and look me in my eyes, and all I saw love. She would give me Eskimo kisses. My heart would just melt.

"Hi, baby," I would say softly.

"Hi Mommy," she would say back.

Those few moments seemed like hours of blissfulness. I look down at her; she looks up at me and smiles at me. My heart skips a beat.

"Good?" I ask.

She giggles and then focuses back on her Italian ice.

"You gonna miss me while you're gone," I ask again.

"Yes," she answered. "You gonna miss me?"

"I miss you already," I said.

I had to look away; tears started to well up in my eyes. I am such a crybaby when it comes to my baby. The fact that I am not going to see her smile for a month is literally breaking my heart. I have never been away from Joy, and a month was too long. I look down and watch her to finishes her Italian Ice. She runs to the nearest trash can and throws away her trash, then she races off to join the other kids. I smile; my baby is so sociable. She freely interacts with the other kids as they run around the park; they climbed the monkey bars, laughed as they slid down the slide, and screamed as they swung on the swings. I am not going to see her enjoy Kennywood or the Pixburg Zoo but watching her smile at this moment brought me so much..., joy.

**"TO MY SISTER, THE** legendary August Schofield," X. said.

He and a few of my friends have gathered together for dinner to celebrate my book tour. Joy is at home with Xavier's girlfriend, Monique.

"I am not a legend," I say modestly.

Xavier ignores me and continues the toast in my honor.

"Too much success on this book tour," my brother continues.

"And to meeting men and getting-,"

"Dominique!" I quickly interrupted her.

She rolls her eyes and chuckles.

"How about: to August, congratulations and much success?" I say, holding up my glass of lemon water.

"Booo," Gina, another one of my colorful friends, says. "To August getting some!"

"To August!" everyone playfully toasts to me.

I shake my head and sip my ice water.

"August, drink something stronger!" Monroe exclaims. "Xavier, we gotta get your sister laid."

"As much as I don't want to think about my sister getting laid, I do agree with you, Roe," X. said to Monroe.

"Don't speak of me in the third person," I said, laughing.

Other than my writing, my friends have a way of keeping me calm. I met them all during my first years in New York. I met Monroe Brown at one of my book signings. She says that she enjoys writing but has never gotten anything published. She works various jobs as a temp in different firms as an accountant. She stands at five-seven, pretty brown skin with round, dark brown eyes. Monroe's dating is somewhat confusing. She may have a boyfriend, but he would live in another country and talk to each other once a month. Whenever she visits her man, she leaves the country for a few weeks and comes back. I love hearing about her trips to Paris or Spain.

My next good friend is Dominique King. Sometimes whenever I have an event to go to, I call Dominique to dress me. Dominque wants to be a stylist. She is a petite laid-back African American woman that is the next Rachel Zoe. Currently, she works for a local magazine and comments on the latest trends. I admire her because she is very, very independent. She asks for nothing, not from men or friends. When it came to relationships, she made commitments, but she did not tolerate nonsense. He must have a steady job. It doesn't have to be a fancy job, but steady. She didn't tolerate emotional men or clingy men. I loved her for that. Next bosom buddy of mine is Clare Baker; she works as a customer service rep at an insurance firm. She is the oldest of the bunch. Like my other girlfriends, she is beautiful, with rich brown skin, and she wore her hairstyle in that Halle Berry style pixie. She hates her job and dreams of owning her own business as a caterer but has yet to put together a flier, a menu, or host some kind of appetizer tasting. Always in good spirits, Clare knows where to get the best takeout food. Her relationship is an on and off-again relationship with a man who gives her the dream's hopes. One minute she breaks up with him only to get chased and get back with him two weeks later.

Tonight, my friends and X came out to celebrate with me. Since we all formed a type of sisterhood, my friends and brother try to get me to meet someone. They worry about me. Based on their comments, they worry that I may end up a spinster. Their fear that I will never have that one great love or get married again. Like X., they fuss about me drifting off to Land of Aug, not venturing out but hibernating in my home. I try to assure them that I am not in the Land of Aug; I am just at home, writing or spending time with Joy.

"I hope that this night is not a get August laid intervention," I said after their toast.

They laugh.

"August, you are too young and too pretty to be alone," Clair said, sipping her wine.

"I'm not alone," I defended myself. "It is hard to date when you have a ten-years old."

"You can be on a date right now," Monroe said.

"Instead, I am hanging out with you," I said with a smirk.

"All right, all right, leave my sister alone," X said, intervened.

"Thank you," I said, smiling.

"Now, let's get to the reason why we are here," Clare beings, "to celebrate the success of August, I read your book, and it was excellent."

I smile. I watch as the others nod their head.

"Thank you," I said.

My friends and X are my true critics. They would tell me the truth about my work.

"And you wrote this in one night," Clare asks, looking over my book.

I had given my friends a free copy.

"Yes,"

"So, tell us about this tour; where is your first stop?" Dominique asked.

"Actually, two days from now, here in Manhattan. The next one is in California. I have never been out of the East Coast!"

Chuckles went through our table.

"Our little August is growing up," X said playfully, crying like a proud parent.

"August, don't turn around," Dominique said softly. "But Miles Palmer is looking at you."

"At me," I questioned in a soft tone.

My eyes watch my brother, Clare's, Monroe's, and Dominique's.

"I noticed him watching for some time," Dominique said.

Xavier cranes his neck to see who exactly had been watching.

"Don't make it obvious," she expressed in a loud whisper.

Maintaining her composer then she smiles at me.

"He's very handsome," he informs.

"Can I look," I ask.

I wait for Dominique to give me a signal. Before she could answer, her eyes widened.

"He coming over this way, be cool," she said with stern eyes.

I sip my ice water and anxiously wait. Miles Palmer is an editor and chief of *Kirby Howard* magazine. *Kirby Howard* is a literary magazine that reviews and critics any artist's new works, such as artwork, to fashion designers' newest fashion line and literature *Kirby Howard* has reported and critic it. It has been compared to the *New Yorker*; however, the difference between the New Yorker and *Kirby Howard* is that the staff at Kirby Howard has more of an urban appeal. Kirby Howard's critics can make or break an artist's career, from how they are interview to their works. Miles Palmer has critiqued all of my work. Thankfully so far, I have been considered a good writer, just a good writer. I know that I need to write a book where people are moved by my work, like the *Great Gatsby* and other literary classics.

When he finally approaches our table, I look up at him. We had never met. I had no idea what he looked like. I have no idea if he is old or young. If he was black or white, tall or short, but as I look upon him, I am immediately taken back, calling him handsome is an understatement. This man is absolutely gorgeous. The first thing I noticed is his eyes. His eyes were the color of aquamarine, and his skin was the color caramel. He is a black man with blue eyes.

"Excuse me," he said.

His voice is a contraction to his beautiful face. His voice is soft but masculine; smooth. He grins politely, he looks at my friends, then he looks at me. His aquamarine eyes almost hypnotized me.

"You're August Schofield,"

"Yes," I answered.

"I enjoy your work," he said.

"Thank you," I reply, finally breaking away from the trance.

The five-second silence is awkward. I don't know what to say to him, and it is very hard to look at him. I sat nervously, wondering what he wanted. Is it just to tell me how much he likes my work?

"Would you like to sit down," Monroe asks, quickly winking at me. "We are here celebrating the release of August's new book."

I watched Miles shoot a glance at Xavier, who happens to be sitting next to me. He must have thought that he is my boyfriend.

"He's not her man," Monroe said with a smile.

I sigh; Monroe's flirtation games can be somewhat annoying. Monroe summons the waiter to our table, but Miles out his hand up to stop him.

"I'm not able to stay, but I just wanted to come over to personally say that I am a fan. I heard of the latest work, and I am intrigued. If it is not too much trouble, I be honored if we sit down for an interview."

I grin.

"Sure, get in touch with my assistant, and we can set something up."

For the first time, I actually like saying, my assistant. Quickly I thought of my assistant, who is all smiles in her pretty cardigan, taking a message from Miles Palmer.

"Okay," he replied.

"It was nice meeting you," I said.

"Likewise,"

We wait until he leaves before we say anything.

"August, he likes you," Dominique said.

"No, he's a reporter. My new book is out. He is going to tear me to shreds." I said, sipping my water.

"August, relax," Xavier said to me.

The ladies glanced at my brother. He grins then eats his appetizer.

"Xavier, did he not look at her?" Monroe asks. "If you don't take him, I will."

"Nope, no, you won't," Dominique quickly said. "This is August time; you have your man across the ocean; let August have her man."

"Um, he's not my man!" I quickly said.

"Oh, relax," Monroe said, sipping her drink.

I take a deep breath. Monroe scratched her hair. which is a wig, moves from side to side. Monroe, as sweet as she is, thinks she is absolutely Carrie Bradshaw fabulous. She wears cute little cocktail dresses, but they are too small. She gets her hair done in a beautifully styled wig or sew-in weave, but we can see the new growth of her natural hair after a month. The idea that she could take my man is not to insult me but to let the table know how fabulous she is. Dominique, my bodyguard, is quick to remind her that she is not that fabulous, and when it's not their season to shine, and they try to steal the thunder from a person, Dom will stop that plan too. I sat at the table, embarrassed at the jokes. I just want to eat grilled shrimp with rice pilaf, drink ice water, and go home. My brother senses my aloofness.

"Listen Lindas," Xavier says, smiling. "Whether Pretty Boy likes my sister or not, we are here to celebrate her."

"Leave it to her big brother to stop any opportunity for her to get some." Clare joked.

"I'm the oldest," I said.

No one heard me; they talked among themselves.

"Anyway, I need to write my Gatsby," I said, with hopes of bringing the attention back to writing. "Did you get Gatsby, Claire?"

With Clare's review, did she see my Gatsby like Adam did? I haven't heard anything from the papers saying that this book captures the essence of the Great Gatsby.

"August, breath," Dominique coaxes. "You are the Zora Neale Hurston. You are Toni Morrison-,"

"F. Scott Fitzgerald!" I exclaim.

I look at Clare; she chuckles; why everyone else rolls their eyes.

"Don't laugh, if I can have that one great masterpiece, my Great Gatsby-,"

I faded out. I close my eyes. I mentally leave, leaving my friends behind. I am lost in my favorite book in the world, *The Great Gatsby*. Words cannot describe the admiration that I have for that book. I think I have maybe five copies of the book, with different footnotes. To be established as one of the world's best authors because of one book. To me, *The Great Gatsby* represents one word: power. You are powerful if you are an established person. Claiming your first love in the face of her husband while wearing a pink suit. Showing him and her that I am The

Great Gatsby, and at the end of the night, when you close your eyes for the last time, we truly see your greatness, because of your hope. Nick is my favorite of all the characters because even though he did not have social standing or the money to make him as great-society standards, he had the most class.

I looked at my friends who were talking among themselves; I sat back, closed my eyes, and imagined a modern-day great Gatsby. I can see the women wearing vintage clothes that are chic yet classy and the men in their tailored suits. What would be the issue, what would their problems be? I open up my eyes and see Tommy sitting at a table across from me. He smiles and gives a slight wave. Then points to his head. I grin slowly and inhale. Quickly I looked at my friends trying to keep up with their conversation, but I heard nothing. I see their lips moving and their mouths smiling, and their eyes dancing as they entertain each other with their tales and comparing similar stories. With Tommy sitting across from me, I want to go home and write. I watch as Tommy moves away from the table. Appearing suddenly are four people, there are two men and two women. They are sitting down, eating, dining, and enjoying each other's company. They were beautiful people. They are well dressed, and their demeanor spoke of sophistication. Their conversation looks interesting.

At this moment, I want to be at their table. I see one of the beautiful people laughing. Their laugh is infectious and contagious,

*What's funny?* I asked myself.

Then I see that everyone at the table laughs along with their friend. One of them looks at me, a woman. She has light brown, almost hazel-colored eyes. Her skin is the color of copper. She wears her jet-black hair pulls back into a bun. Her features are striking; she has an exotic look. Sitting beside her is a man. His dark skin looks smooth like oil, and his eyes look like a dark pool of an intriguing abyss; you wanted to get lost in them, and you did not want to be found. His apparel is well put together as if he is someone from Gentlemen's Quarterly, wearing a tailored suit that looks like silk. He also had a goat-tee. I slowly inhale then exhale. There is just something about a man in a goat-tee that makes me want to go…, ahhhh. The beautiful woman of copper looked at the distinguished gentleman; she whispers something to him; he chuckles, then he looks at me. My heart stops. Tommy suddenly reappears; this time, he stands behind them. I see the characters, my next book.

*August,* I hear my name being called faintly.

The beautiful ones are calling me.

*August,*- they said again.

The second gentleman is dangerously handsome. He has dark brown smoldering eyes. Unlike the distinguished gentleman, he is not as well kept, but he well dressed. He is wearing all black, and his dark hair is tousled. There is a laid-back and reserve quality about him. I watched him sip his drink, and then I noticed the ring on the ring finger of his right hand; it is gold with a sapphire stone. As he sets his glass down, he looks directly at me and holds my attention for a moment. Slowly he turns to face his left-my right- and listens to the woman that was talking to him. By his vacant expression, I could tell that he is not interested in what she is talking about, but at the risk of not being rude, he listened, nodding his head letting her know that he is all ears.

She woman looks like an Italian goddess. Her style is trendy and stylish. She wears her dark hair in a bob style haircut, and her green eyes look like peridot stone. Her coral-colored dress made her olive-colored skin look almost bronze.

"August!" someone calls my name.

"Hmm," I replied.

"August,"

Someone touched my hand, it is Monroe, and I look at her; she is laughing at me. I look at Xavier; he chuckles; he looks at me confused. Dominique laughs.

"Where were you?" she asked with a chuckle.

I chuckle embarrassedly,

"I, ah, zoned out."

"Thinking about that reporter?" Monroe asks.

"What?"

Playfully jeers go through the tables. I quickly stood up.

"I need to go," I said.

"August-," Xavier said.

"I have to write," I said.

"Write?" they asked. "August, we didn't order our dinner."

"I know, I know," I said, "but I-," I stammered. "I just gotta go."

I quickly ran out. Just as soon as I reach the outside. I hear Xavier running after me.

"August!" he called out.

I turn to him.

"X, I gotta go," I said, still walking away. "I have to write."

"Aug, wait-," he grabs my arm. "What's wrong?"

"Nothing," I answer.

He looks at me with intense eyes, not buying my nothing.

"I just got an idea, and I need to go write."

I need that escape again. Just me and my characters, and as interesting as the beautiful ones seemed, this book just might be my Great Gatsby.

"Can't this wait until after dinner?" X. asks.

I let out a sigh.

"We in there to celebrate you." He put his arms around me.

I look away. X. chuckles.

"No, it can't wait; that is why you're August Schofield."

I grin.

X always understands.

"Come on, let me walk you home."

"No, I'm okay-," I protested.

"August, I am not going to let you walk home this time of night. Plus, look, you going the wrong way."

I looked at the street sign and realized I was heading in the wrong direction. My brother shakes his head and laughs. He takes his jacket off and places it around my shoulders.

"What am I going to do with you?" X. said, laughing.

"Just love me," I said.

His actions are why no one realizes that I am the big sister, and he is the little brother. But I savor this moment.

**"IS MY BABY PACKED?"** X. asks, rummaging through my refrigerator.

"Yes, X. she is packed, and she will be ready tomorrow."

"Why don't you have any food?" he asks, sounding frustrated.

"I am leaving for tour; you taking my baby away from me."

"Right, sorry. And don't start with your antics; let go of the apron strings. Your baby will be fine. I'm hungry."

"I'll order a pizza."

I go upstairs to change my clothes and order a pizza. When I came to return, I found X eating a peanut butter and jelly sandwich and watching television. I sat down next to him.

"What happened at the restaurant?" he asks very directly.

"Nothing," I answer, trying to be vague. "I just started brainstorming, and I-, you know The Land of Aug," I said evasively. "How's the bookstore?"

"Don't change the subject," he said.

I look away. He finishes his sandwich then turns off the television. He looks over at me. His eyes are trying to read mine.

"Don't try to read me," I said snap. "I am writing, and you know how I get, Land of Aug, remember."

"Is that all?" he asked suspiciously.

I nod my head and begin to push back my cuticles; glad I have a nail appointment tomorrow.

"You zoned out as soon as we started teasing you about that reporter."

I look up from my nails at him. X's eyes are intense. Quickly I focus my attention back on my nail bed.

"And you left when he was mentioned again." X. finished.

"That didn't bother me," I said.

"What then?"

"Nothing, X., I just want to write."

"It's okay to be found attractive. You're not ugly." He said with a chuckle.

"I am not having this conversation,"

He ignores me,

"And it is okay for you to like someone."

"Xavier, I do not have time to date right now-,"

"Don't use Joy as a crutch," he told me with a scolding yet a concerning look in his eyes.

"X.," I snapped. "I want to write."

"Okay, okay," X. surrenders. "Take me The Land of Aug."

I sigh and begin to tell him about the beautiful ones. I tell my brother about the beautiful ones and how elegant they looked, timeless like The Great Gatsby.

"I saw them?" I said, smiling.

"You saw them," he asked, not in a doubtful sense but in a way that he is showing interest, and he is just as fascinated with them as I.

"Who were they?"

"I don't know," I said. "But I need to write so I can find out who they are. Maybe I should cancel the book tour."

"August, you can't cancel the tour," Xavier said.

"Why not,"

"Because you have fans waiting for you, and you don't want to let them down."

"They would understand," I said, looking away. "What if I did like how Willie Wonka did his chocolate-,"

"August!"

"Listen, X, okay, I can autograph so many books, okay, and whoever gets the autograph can have dinner with me. That way, there is a time limit, and during the time, I can write."

"August," Xavier said, somewhat tired and frustrated. "You can't cancel the book tour. The dates are all set, okay?"

There is a knock at the door. It is the pizza. For a moment, Xavier and I ate pizza and talked. We talk more about the beautiful ones. What do they do, what are their dreams? Who do they love? I think of the Italian goddess. I will name her Alexandria. She is a fickle beauty, always chasing a dream or a possibility. She is in love with the one that is dangerously handsome. His reserve demeanor is fascinating to her. He is a closed book that she wants to open and read. His name is David, one of the most desirable men in the city. He is always wearing dark colors that complimented his somber nature. He is serious; his mother used to call him Papa because of his old soul. David is also a gentleman; he never curses around a lady and always acknowledges her presence whenever she enters a room. He likes Alexandria; she is interesting, her unpredictable and energetic ways make him smile, but he is not looking for a commitment. The distinguished gentlemen, I will call him, Mark. He is a high-power litigator, always having the case won. He knows the ins and outs of the law. He is the go-to man for any legal issue. Power is his middle name.

Last but not least is the beautiful copper girl. Her name is Olivia. Olivia is an event planner, one of the best in the city. She arranges elegant gatherings for the city elite. Like David, she is quiet but likes to laugh. She is a lady that does not want to marry, and she is much the object to men's desires.

"August," Xavier said.

"Yes," I answered, yawning.

"Go to bed now," he instructed. "Your eyes are red, and your voice is hoarse."

"Okay," I surrender.

I lie back on the couch,

"Do you like that idea, like the Willie Wonka?"

"Good night, August."

He kisses me on my forehead, and I watch him leave.

"Good night,"

# 3

**AS I UNPACK, MAYA** comes to my suite to give me the day's agenda. I am to be at a bookstore around ten a.m. for a book signing, and then I had an interview with some morning talk show. And to my surprise, I received an invitation to a writer's party that is given by television personality Darnell Simpson. African- American woman originally from Kentucky, she studied law at Yale, worked as a lawyer for nearly twenty- years, but somehow found herself in front of a camera, being the over friendly yet sweet television personality. In my opinion, Ms. Simpson is a woman with too much time and money on her hands. Although I do admire her because she is known for her contribution to numerous charities. For example, she donates time and money to children with special needs. She is a firm believer in education by helping the underprivileged youth with their college tuition. She helps raise money for presidential campaigns. When you see her, you see the money. Who is she going to donate to, and how much? Why did she invite me to her party? Darnell is an avid reader. She reads good literature, classics like Steinback, Faulkner, Morrison. Literature that takes almost ten years for the author to complete it and when you read it. Every year she hosts a party for the top ten best-sellers of that year and as well as the legendary authors. Also at her parties there are avid readers, socialites, investors, people you want to impress.

This personal invitation is shocking. I never considered myself to be considered by the legendary

Darnell Simpson. I am still waiting to write my literary classic.

Maya stands next to me as I look over the invitation making sure I do not miss reading something. I keep looking at my name on the invitation.

"The Darnell Simpson," I asked, somewhat taken back.

Maya smiles at me.

"She left a personal note, saying considering the book tour that if you are not able to make it, let her know, asap," Maya said. "It's not until the end of the month. Your schedule permits it,"

I shake my head no,

"I don't belong in the room with those legends," I said.

"Are you serious?" Maya asked. "You debuted at number one,"

"Yeah, but Darnell is known to associate with the rich and educated, like Warren Buffet; I am a single mother with an active imagination."

I walked to the window to see the beautiful view of California. It looks like a city of gold. While I'm here, I want to sightsee, like a walk on the Hollywood Walk of Fame. Drink the California lattes; maybe they taste better out here, and of course, something for Joy."

"Oh, and by the way, Miles Palmer of Kirby Howard is asking for an interview."

I almost shudder at his name. I can see his beautiful yet piercing eyes reading my words, critiquing my style. Miles Palmer is dangerous when it comes to Literature; he knew it well. He studied the greats. I wonder if he was invited to Darnell Simpson's party. He said that he admired my work, but with him, admiring can be a basic word. If I avoid him, maybe he will give up and critique someone else. And as great as I want to be, I rather get lost among the great ones than being interviewed by Miles Palmer.

"Don't return any of his calls," I instruct Maya.

"Why?" Maya asks.

"Because I don't want to be interviewed by him," I said. "He's lethal."

"Really?" Maya questions.

"Yes, he is the Anna Wintour of Literature."

"You are a good writer. What negative thing can Miles Palmer say? You are fabulous, you are awesome-,"

"I am not the little white girl in *The Help*." I snap.

Maya looks at me with a blank stare. I inhale and then exhale.

"I'm sorry," I said. "Not that I am a private person, and I don't spend my days doing faux soul searching; I just know what is best for me and my career."

Maya grins, accepting my apology. I smile back.

"How long am I in California for?" I asked, pouring myself a glass of water.

"Two weeks, then off to Dallas, Texas for only two days, and then Chicago, for a week, and Pittsburgh,"

"Pittsburgh?" I asked with a smile. "Joy is in Pittsburgh with my brother Xavier."

Maya smiles.

"Yeah, you are being honored with a coffee. Carter's Books, a small bookstore that recognizes its celebrities. She has all kinds of things named after hometown heroes. Michael Keaton Pound Cake, August Wilson- Omelets, she wants to name a coffee after you."

I grin.

"That is beyond awesome, The Schofield Latte, hazelnut okay, tell them hazelnut,"

"I know, I know," she chuckles, going through her Blackberry phone.

"Let's get you to your book signing."

I nodded my head and pull out an outfit from the closet that I had unpacked. Maya's drops when she looks at the all-black clothing.

"Are you serious?" she asked.

I give her a small slight nod.

"You really wear all black? Have you noticed that it is like a hundred degrees outside? You are in California, and it's the summer,"

"It's not summer; it's late spring. And don't judge me. Janet Jackson did it; she was in control with the rhythm nation. I do it; I am considered a nut case."

She looks back at my closet with a sigh,

**"AUGUST, LET' SEE, BABE."** I hear Dominique say.

I stand in the dressing room in Rodeo Drive, looking at my outfit. A little black number that can definitely get me breakfast at Tiffany's. A strapless wide-leg jumpsuit, there is a type of shimmer to the material that gives the outfit a glamorous look. I inhale and exhale, actually liking the outfit.

After much convincing and practically arguing with my pretty assistant, I decided to go to Darnell Simpson's Writers Party. So I flew Dominique out to

California. Maya, Dominique, and I went shopping along Sunset Blvd. Because I think Maya is on a mission to make me as pretty as she, with the cute cardigans and pearls and nothing black and chic, I need Dominique to be that bodyguard to instruct her that August Schofield does what she wants to do. When it comes to wearing the color black, there is no real reason why I wear so much black. I am making some kind of statement, and I am not depressed. There is a chic elegance. I can wear pearls or diamonds. With my hair pinned up in a bun and Little Black Dress, I can channel my inner Audrey. With a pair of black slacks and a type of boat neck shirt, I am never overdressed or underdressed. Call my apparel a safety net because I always land on top. I tried to explain this concept to Maya.

"Well, if you ask me," she began. "Black drowns you out; it's basic and boring,"

Dominique looked at her,

"You like to playthings safe. You don't want to stand out, nor do you want to fade into the back," Maya commented as I looked over an outfit.

I gave Maya a smirk, ready for Dominique to take her down.

*Get her, Dom.* I said to myself.

But Dominique did not get her.

"Black is her signature, every artist has their signature," Dominique said.

The girls wait for me to come out of the dressing room. I step out, and the ladies smile.

"I love it," Dominique states.

I look at Maya; her pretty brown eyes stare at me. I grin.

"You are more than Carrie Bradshaw-," she says smiling.

"Of course, she is," Dominique states, cutting her eyes at Maya. "She's August Schofield."

**"DO YOU KNOW WHO** is going to be at this party? Did you get a heads up on the guest list?" I ask Maya.

"No, just the invitation," she answered me. "I can find out.

I let out a sigh,

"No, it's not important."

**I HAD MY FILL OF** shopping. I think I spent more money in one boutique than I have in the past year, but I love jewelry. I love diamonds, rubies, emeralds, sapphires, Swarovski Crystals. After I got what I needed, Dominique and Maya went shopping more. I went to the hotel lounge to write. I sit down in the far back, out of view from everyone. This is how I like it. I'm not shy but, when I am writing, I don't want any distractions.

"Hi, I'm Katie, your server; what can I start you off with today?"

"Katie, I am going to be here for a while, so for starters, can I have a tall glass of ice water, and do you have grilled chicken sandwiches?"

She nods her head,

"Okay, a grilled chicken sandwich with provolone cheese, extra mushrooms, lettuce, no tomatoes, please."

"Okay," she said with a grin, then walked away.

I turn my laptop on and prepare myself to write. I have my journal. I am ready to write- *The Beautiful Ones*; this is going to be my Gatsby. I am going to be up there with Fitzgerald. I close my eyes and try to see the four beautiful people that I saw a week ago. I need issues; what are their issues? With the Great Gatsby- Jay wanted Daisy; did the beautiful ones want someone who they can't have?

Mark, he marries Sandy. Sandy is perfect; she is a beautiful woman who is the perfect wife. She comes from a fine pedigree. As lovely as Sandy is, Mark is not in love with her. He did not love Sandy. They have been married for five years, and now they are receiving pressure from both sides of the family to start a family. Mark doesn't want children. He doesn't want any obligations to Sandy because when it is time to leave-

*Leave where is he going?* I asked myself.

Katie brings out my water and sits it on the table. I look up and see Tommy sitting beside me. I take a deep breath.

*Hi*, he said.

I don't know how to respond.

*You don't have to speak; I'm in right here.* He points to his head.

*Why wouldn't Mark live, Sandy? She's perfect.* I thought.

*Perfection doesn't mean love*, he answered.

*So then why marry her?*

*Society rules*, he answers.

Society, a dangerous concept. Money rules everything. For the love of money is the root of all evil. If one had money, they could rule the world, but the question is class, like Gatsby's East Egg and West Egg. In *The Great Gatsby*, in my opinion, had no class. He was old money, but he was boorish and crude. To cheat on his wife with a woman with no class, to me, is no class. Nick, had class; he was a gentleman. Gatsby was trained to have class. He was trained to be a gentleman. He was trained in his social manors. Jordan had no class. Her beauty was undefinable, but her way of life is not classy. Gatsby was about when old money meets new money. Can old money and new money coincide together? Tom was intimidated by Gatsby's new money. His new brought about change, and Tom was not comfortable with change. Mark's education and classic demeanor distinguished him and set him apart from the rest of his peers to allow him to be new money. Sandy is old money, and to have Sandy chose him; is an honor.

*But who does he love?* I ask myself. *Was he in love with his work?*

I shake my head no, answering my own question. He loves someone. Someone who is not of them, money old or new. A woman who has class and grace. Mark loves her gentle nature, and he loves the way she smiled. She is a soft beauty. Her face is not covered in cosmetics.

"When I am established, I will come for you," he said to Soft Beauty.

Standing outside in an abandoned park underneath the diamonds in the sky, they hold each other. Tomorrow, Mark will marry Sandy, and he will leave this girl, Soft Beauty, heartbroken. She sobs softly in his arms.

"Please understand," he pleads, trying to understand. "This move will benefit my family. Doors will be opened for us, and when I accomplish what I need, then I will come back to you,"

Mark dries her tears. He can tell that she doubts every word.

"We won't have any children," he vows.

"What?" Soft Beauty asks him, almost offended at his remark. "How is that possible?"

Mark hesitates to answer.

"I will just tell Sandy that children are not an option right now," he suggests.

Soft Beauty pushes herself away from him.

"I have to go," she says.

"Promise you'll wait for me," he begs.

She shakes her head slowly then backs away.

"I can't-," cries back tears.

She turns around and runs away.

"Is everything okay," a voice asks, startling me.

I look up and see Katie standing before me.

"I noticed that you haven't touched your sandwich."

I look at the grilled chicken sandwich. I don't remember her setting the plate of food down. Quickly I cut my eyes to my left to see if Tommy is still next to me; he is. I look back at Katie.

"I'm okay, thank you," I say, smiling.

She smiles,

"Let me know if you need anything," she said, then walked away.

I slowly inhale and then slowly exhale.

*August,* Tommy began,

*There's no dilemma,* I said to him. I wouldn't wait for him either.

Tommy looks at me as if I am missing something.

*Write,* he instructs me.

I focus my attention back on my laptop. My heart is breaking. I can no longer dwell on the non-existing love triangle of Mark, Sandy, and Jennifer.

*Who's next?* I asked myself.

Olivia. I remember Olivia, Mark and she seemed close at the restaurant, they are good friends-Philo Love. Sandy is not intimidated by their Philo Love, but she wants the same affection. Once again, Mark is shutting out his wife. Is there something about Sandy where no one wants to love her? No, because Sandy is great. She is wonderful.

*Why are you so loyal to Sandy?* Tommy asks.

*Stability-,* I answer.

*Stability-,* He asks.

*After a long day of conquering giants, would you not want to come home to peace and quiet? To someone who isn't always arguing over petty and insignificant matters.*

*Sounds real ideal-,* Tommy said. *But August, that is not realistic. You can come home to children crying or sick. There may be devastating news,*

*I know, I know all that-,* I said, *but when you have peace, those storms are like mild rain falls. When there is peace, you can witness a storm and all its destruction, but it doesn't matter to you because there is peace within you.*

*And Sandy has peace?* Tommy asked.

As much emotional turbulence is going around her, is she at peace? She has a man that doesn't love her; he is using her for social connections.

*She knows that he'll benefit from her connections. Mark is not ungrateful.* I state.

*August, you, of all people, know how to survive in a storm.* Tommy said.

I nod my head. It almost killed me when Joy's light almost went out. I shake my head, trying not to think of those days. I inhale and exhale.

*What does Olivia want?* Tommy asked.

*Freedom,* I quickly answered, shocked by my sudden response.

*She is not free?* He asks.

I can't answer.

I am getting the understanding that Olivia is a complicated individual. She wants life, and she wants it abundantly. She is not ruthless, but she is clever, and she is intelligent. She had stood by Mark's decision to marry Sandy, although she knew that it was wrong. Olivia is beauty is spellbinding. Men have followed her just to tell her that she is beautiful. She has many, many admirers, men of high nobility, men with great wealth who wanted her hand, but she refused.

"I belong to no man," is her saying.

*What is her hang up on marriage?* Tommy asks. *What is the bondage?*

*There are rules when it comes to marriage.* I explained.

*Rules?*

*Rules. You need to, well, you should be mindful of your spouse's needs. Quality time, how you spend money, etc...., etc....,* I said, rolling my eyes.

*And that is a bad thing?* Tommy asked with a chuckle.

*No, not if you have the right one who appreciates your quality. When you're free, you're under no obligation to give anyone your time. You can run as fast as you can and fly high in the sky. Sleep wherever your head falls.*

She watched Mother's suffer from the bondage. Daddy questioned any sparkle that was in Mother's eyes. Smiling was not optional. What does one have to smile about? Mother smiled because of love. She loved to watch Baby Olivia smile and laugh, but Father didn't understand the liberty they had inside them. Olivia and her family were poor, hungry, and cold, and what you don't understand frightens you. Father saw their liberated spirits as a threat, so he did all he could to break it. He beat it out of them whenever he saw their spirit rose up. He would starve it.

Finally, after being a slave to Father's oppression for so many years, Mother died. Olivia was fifteen years old. She refused to stay with her father in fear that he would kill her. She moved out and lived on her own. Olivia didn't worried about eating because she went days without food. She didn't worry about sleeping because she had many sleepless nights. Surviving was not questioned because she's a survivor. All that was important was her freedom. No one will ever tell her to stop smiling.

*Does she hate men?* Tommy asked.

*No, she has Mark; he lets her be her and David.* I answered.

*David?* I said his name in shock.

Where does David come into the picture? David seems so solemn. He is somber; his serious demeanor is mysterious and sexy.

*David doesn't want a commitment,* Tommy reminded me. *What is his problem?*

Serious people don't have time for commitments. They are too busy being serious. I said.

He enjoys Alexandria's company, but she is for mere pleasure. She is not someone who he would consider settling down with; if he settled down. If marriage were to be considered, it would be for business; a business arrangement.

Considering these circumstances, David is coming upon a stage in his life where he needed a woman in his life to make the social appearances. Being the most eligible bachelor is no longer amusing to him. If marriage is the next alternative, it would be strictly business. She would be on his arm for social appearances. She would make a happy home, sex on a regular.

*Pig!* I snapped.

They can have separate rooms if she wishes. As long as she is available for him to snuggle with at night. She must have a brain. She must know business. Someone he can leave his estate to. Alexandra is pleasurable for David in the evenings; she would not be a suitable wife. Olivia would be more apt. Her business mind would only increase his already abundant fortune.

"I belong to no man," Olivia said to him one day.

At a fundraiser, they danced on the ballroom floor.

"Your defiance against matrimony is endearing," he said to her. "But look at this as a business opportunity,"

"Business,"

"I have lots of money," he says bluntly, "You need business investors."

"So, marry you for money," she laughs. "Can't you find some fickle girl to do that?"

"She would spend my money. You, I know you wouldn't run through my money."

"Why me?"

"Why not?" he asked. "You are someone I know, someone I trust, we can respect each other's personal space, and we can meet each other's needs," he gently caressed her cheeks.

"No, I won't be known as Olivia; me, I would be known for Mrs. you. When people see me, they will expect to see you. There is no freedom in that,"

"Olivia, where is the bondage in being considered a team?"

"Because with a team, you have to work together," She said to him. "I have to meet you where you are at, always. Going to galas, pose as the loving and happy wife. Hosting a dinner party, be on your arm. That isn't freedom. Worried about your money, make Mark the executor of your estate. In the event of your demise, your money will be safe."

"I will be there for you too," David said. "If you need me on your arm for social events, I will pose as the devoted and loving husband. And money, you never have to worry again."

"I don't want to be bound to your money. I have my own money,"

"But when you are on top, you are free." He told her. "You're not on top yet, I know the right people, I can introduce them to you, and before you know it, you'll be one of the most successful and be the richest woman in the world."

Financial freedom did entice Olivia.

"What about our nighttime," she asked.

"I expect that, as much as you do." He said without emotion.

"Monogamous,"

David chuckles as his coal dark eyes pierce into Olivia's eyes.

"Do you really think that I would allow a wife to be unfaithful, no matter what the terms of the agreement are?"

"I don't love you," she says to him boldly. "I don't want to be with just one man, especially if I don't love him."

David looked away.

"I wouldn't be with anyone else," he said.

"Then I would belong to you, and my freedom is none,"

David sighs: he looked into her eyes again,

"You know me; you have known me for many years. I am an upstanding man."

His demeanor is gentle. David looks Olivia in the eyes.

"I am also your friend. I would not put you in an uncompromising position. I will not make you feel trapped."

"What if I decided to leave, that I want out-,"

"I will draft up a prenuptial agreement if that would be the case, but trust me, I don't think you will want out."

Olivia ponders on his words for a moment.

"This will really hurt Alexandria," Olivia comments.

David shrugs his shoulders,

"This may, but I am sure that she will understand that my rejection is nothing personal."

*He is so unruffled-* I said.

I see Olivia's eyes look for some kind of emotion in David's eyes. She can use the money that David is willing to provide.

Word spread fast that Olivia and David are getting married. Alexandria is furious. Rage fills her heart, and wrath flows through her veins. She loves David. Alexandria had hoped that maybe one day he would consider her for marriage. But he had told her that he was not one for commitments. However, now, he is getting married- to Olivia? A bitter and cold woman. She doesn't love him. When did he fall in love with her? Alexandria's rage caused her vision to become blurry, and the only thing that she can see is red. How dare he just drop her on the side of the road as if she is trash? She has set in her heart to kill him. She will wait until the right moment, all of them, Mark, Olivia, and him, David, when they least expect it.

*Don't let them see you coming,* I heard him whisper.

Like the last time, I found myself lost in thought. It is like an explosion, writing until my fingers hurt, taping rapidly away at my laptop. Tommy at my side, he whispers in my ear:

*Don't let them see you coming.*

As excited as I am to be in my world, I see that The Beautiful Ones are not beautiful. There is nothing attractive about their real nature. They are cunning and crafty, always scheming and always trying to find ways to get over it. They are beautiful on the outside with their designer clothes and glamour, but their insides are ugly.

**I AM AWAKENED BY** the telephone. I sit up and try to recall why the phone is ringing and where I am. I look at my surroundings. I am in my suite. I cover my face with my hands and sigh. The phone still rings.

"Yes," I say, answering the phone.

"Ms. Schofield," said the voice, "This is the front desk with your morning wake up call,"

I sigh.

"Thank you," I said, then hung up the phone.

I look at the clock; it reads five a.m. My body aches: I feel beaten as if I did a hard day of cardio. I have a headache. I lay back down in the bed. I am not about to move. I try to remember last night and why I am so sore. I was with them, The Beautiful Ones. I had become them, a beautiful one. They called my name:

"August," I heard them say, "August,"

Their beautiful appearance was lovely yet immorally seductive. Mark was someone you wanted on your side. He was an influential lawyer that saw that justice was met. Olivia wanted to be an advocate of those whose spirits didn't fly. David, his calm demeanor was somewhat disturbing, yet he was intrigued because he was generous. Alexandria, she had her carefree ways. She wants to make you laugh and smile. She wants to love. But how they obtained their beauty, breaking hearts and rules, I knew I could not want to be of them. As I wrote, I was pulled into their beautiful abys. As I wrote, I tried hard to break away from them.

My cell phone rings. I see Joy's face on the screen.

"Hi, baby,"

"Good morning, Mommy," her voice is melodious.

"What are you doing?" I ask

"Watching TV with Uncle X. We're going to the Wave Pool today. I got a new swimming suit."

"Oooh, what color is it?" I asked her.

"Mommy, it's red." Joy said to me as if I was supposed to know. "Mom, did you buy me anything?"

I closed my eyes as my head throbbed.

"Not yet; what do you want," I ask.

Joy tells me her list of must-haves; I sigh as I listen to her.

"Mom," she said. "I went up the mountain,"

"The mountain," I asked.

"Yes, me and Uncle X got in this box and went up the mountain,"

I chuckle,

"The Incline," I said.

"Mom, what did you have for dinner?"

"I had a chicken sandwich; what did you eat?"

"Uncle X, got me a sandwich, and guess what?"

"Hmm," I said, exhausted by her energy.

"It had French Fries and coleslaw on it. I didn't like it, so Uncle X got me McDonald's with chicken nuggets-," Joy stops talking to me.

I hear her talking to someone else, "I'm on the phone-,"

"Hello," my brother gets on the phone.

"X,"

"August, I'm sorry, I didn't know she was on the phone. It is eight am., over here."

"It's okay, Xavier." I said. "it's time for me to get up. I have an early day."

"California is nice?"

"Real nice and sunny," I said with a chuckle.

"It's been rainy here," Xavier says. "August, you sound tired. What time did you get to bed?"

"About two hours ago," I confess.

"Up all night writing," he accuses in a joking way.

"Guilty," I confessed.

"What time is your signing?"

"Not until ten, but I have to do a few other interviews."

"Don't wear yourself out," he instructed.

"I won't,"

I hung up my phone, slowly got out of bed. I need a shower, a hot shower to ease my sore body. As I shower, I think of The Beautiful Ones. It bothers me that

I was with them. I begin to question myself. Am I a shallow person? Am I cunning and crafty?

**I SUBMIT MY WORK TO** Adam with the instructions to call me ASAP. I look at the clock; it reads six am. I am in much need of coffee, with a few extra shots of espresso. There is a knock at the door. I answer the door; it's Maya and in her hands is a tall Hazelnut latte.

"How did you know?" I ask, taking the coffee.

"August Schofield never sleeps," she answers with a chuckle. "I overheard you tell the receptionist to give you a wake-up call."

"Remind me to give you a raise,"

"I called you last night to see if you wanted me to bring your breakfast, but you didn't answer the phone,"

"You called," I asked her.

She nods,

"My phone didn't ring," I state.

Maya shows me her cell phone and shows me the missed calls the times she called me. Three attempts of her calling me. I grin with embarrassment. She looks at my laptop.

"Gotcha," I said.

"August Schofield," she says with a chuckle. "Were you writing all night?"

I nodded as I sip the latte,

"We have a few hours until your interview. I can come back so you can get some sleep?"

"No, I'm up, may as well start my day," I replied.

"All right," she said. "We can go downstairs; they have breakfast, fresh fruit, we can go over the day's agenda."

"Sure,"

I dressed quickly, then slid on a pair of flip-flops and followed Maya to the hotel's dining area. There are all sorts of foods, from fruits, yogurts, pancakes, sausage, bacon, eggs, French toast. I am not in the mood for anything on display. I watch Maya pile food on her plate. I sit at a table that is by a window. Other than a book signing and interview with a magazine company, I had my day free.

"August, we need to RSVP you attending Darnell Simpson's party," Maya says, sitting down with her plate.

"After breakfast, Joy gave me a list of things to buy her," I said, changing the subject. "I want to get everything and have it shipped to my brother's bookstore in New York,"

"Okay," she said. "California is beautiful,"

Maya looks out the window as she bits down on a strawberry.

"Yeah," I said. "It's not New York or Pittsburgh,"

"Are you homesick?"

"No, just ready to get back to the east coast," I answer.

"You are on the top right now; enjoy this,"

"I am enjoying this, but something is missing,"

"A man?" she asked, teasing me.

I frowned my face.

"No, a masterpiece,"

"A masterpiece?" she asked. "Have you read the reviews? Your book is number one,"

"I know, but it is not a masterpiece,"

"I think you're too hard on yourself,"

"I have to be," I said to her. "Hemmingway, Salinger, Toni Morrison, were not mediocre authors. Their works are masterpieces. I need mine. Anyone can write a book, but it's a skill that creates the masterpiece."

"The reviews say that this is your best work yet,"

I shrug and nod my head and sip my latte.

"So, they say," I replied. "But I know I can do better,"

**I AM ESCORTED INSIDE** her home- her grand and luxuries home, a mansion that is practically a mile long. The butler, a little white man, wearing a tuxedo, reminding me of Alfred from Batman. He introduces himself. He is so serious and smug that he almost frightens me.

Together we walk down a long hallway. I look at the photos and décor along the way. Pictures of Darnell Simpson and famous people. Pictures of her doing her charity work. There are paintings along the walls. He opens the two large doors that led to Darnell and said impressively.

"Ms. August Schofield,"

He steps to the side, and I nervously step forward. I am greeted by her majesty. She has a wide and welcoming smile. Quickly, I try to figure out if her smile is fake or if she is really genuine. Her hair is big and curly, her makeup- although too much, is flawless. She wears what looks like five karat diamonds in her ear. Darnell's outfit is very chic. She wore a pair of navy blue wide-leg slacks and a floral blouse. She wears strings of pearls and matching earrings. She had big and curly hair. My eyes quickly look at her guess. The men were dressed, and their women wore pretty dresses and subtle jewelry. At this moment, I am glad that I am wearing my expensive black jumpsuit and precious jewelry that I had purchased in California. To my surprise, there are not a lot of people. Am I late?

"You look very pretty," she says to me. "Welcome to my home and thank you so much for coming."

"Thank you for the invitation," I said humbly, tempted to bow.

"I've read all of your work, and I am a big fan."

I grin and look away bashfully.

"August," Darnell said, taking me out of my pity trance, "let me introduce you to the others."

Bobbie Coleman, an African American novelist. She was awarded the Pulitzer in 1975 for her book, *Red Jade Eyes*, which was the first book I read by her when I was twenty-two. Her writing is somewhat poetic; once you read the work, I mean really read her work, and everything falls into place, from the logic and motivations of her characters to the plot of the story. One can be caught up in her work, become an actual observer, an eyewitness. I have read everything she has written. If I had known that she was here, I would be like a star-struck fan, brought my books, and had her sign them. Walter Poindexter, his work is classic as well. Two of his books became movies, giving the lead actor Oscars. I never read his work before, but I know he is dangerous when it comes to literature. Rochelle Parker, a play write she is called the Female August Wilson. A young African-American writer who is fresh writing controversial plays almost exposes man's stupidity yet showing redemption in them as well. Jack Grayson and Jimmy Peters, two mystery suspense writers. They are accompanied by their wives. Last but not least is Violet Washington, the poet, author, activist, and motivational speaker, that close and personal friend of Darnell Simpson. Like Bobbie, she is a seasoned writer; she has a cool and gentle demeanor.

Here I am, literally in the presence of royalty. As I smiled and introduced myself to everyone, my stomach turned and flipped. I don't want to be here.

"Because the day is so beautiful, we will be having dinner outside," Darnell told me.

I grin.

"August, tell me about yourself," Bobbie requests with a grin.

I slowly inhaled,

"What would you like to know?"

"You're from Pittsburgh, right?" Rochelle asks, smiling. "I have family that way."

"I really enjoy your work," Bobbie says.

"My work?" I ask, shock. "Ms. Coleman, I enjoy your work."

Bobby chuckles.

"Who are some of your inspirations?" asks smiling.

"F. Scott Fitzgerald, Toni Morrison, you," I said, looking away.

"Bobbie always gets the fans!" Jack complains jokingly.

"Write a Pulitzer Prize-winning novel, and you'll get fans too," Jim said laughing.

"Thank you," Bobbie said humbly. "When I first heard of you, I was curious to the fuss. Who is the young girl who has the gift to capture a scene?"

Her words leave me in shock. I never heard of my work describe that what. The way she looks at me, her eyes are intense as if she is waiting for me to tell her a secret, my secrets, but I don't have any. I grin, nodding my head in thanks for the description of my work. I look at Violet; she nods her head in agreement, then sips her wine.

"August, what can I get for you to drink?" Darnell asks me.

"Water will be fine," I told her.

I watch as Darnell leaves to go to another room.

"You have quite a gift to be so young." Bobbie states, "When did you know you want to be a writer?"

"When I was eight," I said.

"The age of great imagination, when make-believe was natural," Violet commented.

"Nowadays, if you had an overactive imagination or the thought of having an imaginary friend, they want to have you committed," Jack says with a chuckle.

I chuckle with him, and I immediately think of Tommy.

"Those make the best writers," Bobbie says, smiling.

Darnell returns with a bottle of water and glass filled with ice. I watch as she poured the bottle for me, then hand it to me with a smile.

"Thank you," I said, smiling.

"August, I must say," Darnell begins, sitting down with us. "I enjoyed all of your books, August. You don't find literature like that anymore. And this book is a success already,"

I casually nod my head.

"Do you have any children?" Violet asks.

"I have a ten-year-old daughter, Joy."

I reach in my purse and pull out a cell phone to pull up my gallery images of Joy. Ooohs and Ahhs go through.

"She is beautiful," they said.

I modestly said thank you as I put my phone away.

"Jack, how are your children?" Violet asked.

"Oh, don't get me started," he complained.

Various chuckles go forth.

"Tony wants to move to Alaska to find himself-whatever that means, and Patty, well, she is a nut case, just like her mother,"

Jack's wife scoffs at his comment but then smiles.

"Patty is eccentric," Jack's wife says.

Again, several chuckles go forth.

"How are the grandchildren, Bobbie," Jack asks.

"Malcolm broke his collarbone jumping off the roof. He had to prove his mother's theory in flying. Turns out that she was right, that he cannot fly,"

Laughs go forth.

"Children," Bobbie says, laughing.

"We are waiting for Rochelle to join the pack," Violet jokes.

"Leave me out of this," Rochelle laughed.

**SOFT JAZZ MUSIC PLAYS** in the background, as the staff place garden salads in front of us. Still sitting outside on a patio, at a table that serves eight, I sit with Darnell Simpson and Literary Royalty. I sip my ice water and listen and chuckled with Darnell Simpson and Literary Royalty as they told war stories about their children, grandchildren, politics and discussed their favorite television drama such as reality T.V., *The Walking Dead Game of Thrones,,* or something on Netflicks. I couldn't relate because my home is in Bikini Bottom.

I sit amazed at how carefree these writers are. Do any of them have anything that they are currently working on, any new material, and if so, do they have writer's block? I am on pins and needles right now, wanting to go back to my hotel and go into that Land of Aug. Except for Rochelle, each of them had published works before I was born. They are seasoned writers, authors. I am sitting here with Literary Royalty; I feel out of my league. I don't want to talk politics, reality T.V., and I don't want to share recipes. And my child is not rambunctious or wild.

I look at the hill that is apart from the grounds. There is a woman, a young girl, she looks like she is at least eighteen or nineteen. She is standing on top of the hill. She wears what looks like a white silk gown; it's a nightgown. The nightgown makes her look almost angelic. She is a beautiful woman, her skin is brown and long black hair was I see an older gentleman walking towards her. By his strong facial features, I can tell that he is Italian. His dark hair is pushed back. He wears a maroon smoking jacket and a black and gold ascot. As she looks up at him, he reaches his hand out to her. He pulls her into him and then wraps his arms around her. He leans in to kiss her, and then he leads her out of sight.

*Who are they?* I ask myself.

I return my attention back to the party and see Tommy sitting in a vacant seat. I grin, he smiles back.

*I'm writing? Now?* I ask mentally.

Tommy shrugs his shoulders in a non-chalet manner.

I sipped my water and picked at my salad. I wanted to know who those people are. By the looks of their appeal, it looks as if they are going to bed.

"Darnell," I lean in and say in a soft tone.

She looks at me with a grin,

"What's over that hill?"

Darnell looks in the direction that I am referring to. She shakes her head, "Nothing," she answers, returning to her meal. "Just vacant land,"

I look at Tommy, and then I look back at the hillside. There is another gentleman, someone new on the hill. A black male, standing at six feet –two inches. He is dressed casually, in jeans and a T-shirt. He appears to be waiting for someone. Within' moments, he joins by another man; he is Italian; not the older Italian. The two shake hands and begin to engage in conversation.

"August," I hear someone call my name.

I turn to whomever it was but then quickly focus my attention back on the hill; the two men are gone.

"August," they call out again.

"Yes," I answer.

Darnell is speaking to me.

"Would you like the smoked salmon or the grilled chicken?" Darnell asks.

I look up and see the staff serving our entrees. I grin.

"The salmon, please," I answer.

The soft jazz continues to play in the background; the staff comes and removes our salads and places our main entrees in front of us, smoked salmon, rice pilaf, and steamed broccoli.

"I'm sorry, I got distracted." I apologize.

"It's all right," Rochelle says, laughing. "We were asking your opinion on the media's outlook on the scandals in Hollywood,"

*Are you kidding?* I want to ask. *Who cares!*

I glance at my watch; it is only six pm. I still have at least four hours of this party before I can make up an excuse to leave.

I grin.

"I really don't know what to say," I reply.

"August doesn't have time to hang out with us," Jimmy Peters says with a chuckle. "She is young. She should be out on the town, enjoying her success,"

"I hear the book tour is successful," Violet says to me with a smile. "Are you enjoying yourself?

"Actually, I haven't seen much of California," I confess. "I have been working on a few things.

"Another book?" Rochelle asks.

I shrugged my shoulders.

"I'm jotting down ideas."

"Watch out, Jack," Darnell warned playfully. "Pretty soon, she will have as many books as you,"

Jack smiles at me approvingly.

"I've read all of your work, and I feel confident enough to speak for everyone here; I am beyond impress."

"Thank you," he said humbly.

"August, do you have any ideas what this next book is about?" Darnell asked.

"Complicated people," I answer. "But I am finding myself at a block,"

"Writer's block is cancer," Walter says, frowning his face.

"Oh, but some cancers are curable," Violet with a grin.

"Keyword; some," Jimmy replied.

"What is your muse," Violet asks.

I shrug, not wanting to answer.

*My muse is not a what but a who, and he is actually sitting beside you.* I want to say.

"I am not stuck on what to do, but I am stuck on understanding my character's motivation," I said. What do you do when you don't get your characters?" I ask.

"What do you mean?" Darnell asks.

"I mean, when you don't understand their motives or when you don't agree with their concepts. Do you stop writing?"

"Never stop writing," Violet said in almost a dramatic way.

As I am about to make a serious offense.

"When it comes to an understanding of your characters," Violet begins, "you must understand that you are not the characters. You may be a type, but you're not the character. Your characters are the alter-ego of you. So, you cannot stop writing because it's your story. The favorite book that I wrote is Washing the Stone, it's my book, because the characters are so-," she stops talking and laughs.

I nodded my head agreeing with her silence, though. I read that book, and that book was something different from what Violet is known for.

"You understand, baby?"

"Yes, ma'am," I said smiling. "Do you ever see your characters or get too involved?"

Several chuckles go forth.

"All the time," they said.

"I see mine in dreams," Walter said to me. "It is crazy; if I am working on a book, I won't get any sleep until I put the book to bed. How ironic, I can go to bed until the book does,"

"You birth characters, like a mother birth a child," Bobbie said.

"It hurts that bad!" I exclaimed.

I've read all of Bobbie's books, but for her characters to put her in that much pain, I almost fell off my seat.

"No," she said with a chuckle. "But when they are created and ready to be developed, I have to push, literally not figuratively.

"Everyone has their way of communicating with their work," Jack replies.

"Yeah, this is coming from the one who writes a book every six months," Walter teases.

"My quantity does not compare to the quality of these legends," he says humbly. He holds his drink to toast Bobbie and Violet. They smile at him, and he holds his glass to me,

"Or the legends to come."

I gasp at the comment. Will I be sitting here in Darnell's backyard twenty years from now with a young writer?

"Thank you," I say humbly. "Everyone here, I am a fan of your works. I read every one of your books."

I look to Darnell,

"Did you know this?"

She grins.

"If F. Scott was alive, he would be here too," Darnell says, smiling.

At this moment, I realize that this party is not just a party, but a party for me. Darnell Simpson doesn't know me, but she still gave me a party to celebrate me and for me to meet my favorite writers. Based on their works, I know that they go off to some land and write. They reside in their imagination.

**TOGETHER IN HER GARDEN,** with our arms linked as if we were old girlfriends, we take a stroll. I loved her garden. The well-groomed and well-manicured garden looks to be a block long. The setting sun gifts me with a bronze and maroon sunset.

"I feel like I am in some kind of tropical paradise," I say softly.

"Ever thinks of moving to California?" Darnell asks.

"I am too in love with my brownstone in New York, but every time I look at a garden, one this beautiful, it's like I'm in another world."

"Then come visit me, any time you want." She says, smiling.

I look at her, shock at her generosity. She has given me a party with Literary Royalty, and now she extends her home to me.

"August, I like you. I have followed your career within the past few years. I must say that your evasive and private demeanor is intriguing. The world wants to know you. Your books, your words draw us in, and you are a curiosity."

I don't know how to respond to what she has said. I inhale and exhale and continue to look at the sunset.

"Where do you see yourself in ten years?" Darnell asks.

"In ten years, I hope to win the Pulitzer, my daughter in college, I like to have a home in Europe- sit on the balcony and write while Joy spends my money at some overpriced boutique,"

Darnell laughs.

"In other words, just live the good life; have the American Dream,"

*The Gatsby concept,* I thought to myself.

As Darnell and I walk, I see the hill. Tommy is sitting on the hill. I see the young girl again. Instead of the older man, she is with the black male.

Where was the one that kissed her? I ask myself.

Looking at the two of them, they look at each other as if they loved each other.

Where is the older guy? I ask myself again.

Then I realize that she isn't wearing the long white gown, a cream-colored dress suit. I see tears falling from her face. My eyes shift to Tommy.

What is going on? I question.

I need to go back to my suite. I have to write. This will be three out of three, the third book I have written in a month.

**ONCE I ARRIVE AT** my hotel suite, I am greeted by Maya.

"So, how was the party?" she asks.

She looks adorable in her drawstring sweatpants and matching tank top. She wears a thin gold necklace with her name on it. Her cute bob hairstyle is pulled back with a thin cream-colored headband. Is she always this adorable?

"Why are you cute at one in the morning?" I ask. "You should be asleep."

"I wanted to go over your agenda for tomorrow," she grins. "You think I look cute?"

"Did you put that outfit together to give me my agenda?" I questioned.

"No," she laughs, "I haven't been to bed yet. How was the party?"

"Nice," I answer as I kick off my shoes and sit down in the love seat.

"Tomorrow morning, you have your interview with Hot Radio 327. The first twenty-five callers get a few autographed book."

I tilt my head back and sigh.

"Okay,"

I sit up and watch Maya go to the bar in my suite to fix me a glass of water. I grin as she hands the glass to me.

"Thank you,"

"So, who was at the party?" Maya asks.

"All of the Literary Royalty," I answered. "Bobbie Colman, Walter Poindexter, Rochelle Hill, Jack Grayson, Jimmy Peters, and Violet Washington."

"Heavy hitters indeed," she said. "Miles Palmer also called in?"

I shake my head,

"Let's schedule the interview; he can meet you in Dallas."

"What else is the agenda for tomorrow," I asked.

"Harper's books at ten," she said. "I will be here at six?"

"Yep," I answered, "See you tomorrow,"

I walk Maya out. Immediately, I jump in the shower; I think about that young woman. Although her eyes are tender, they were serious. There is a look for each man in her life. With the older gentleman, her eyes are tender, as if she is devoted to him. With the younger

Italian man, her eyes are serious and intense. With the black male, her eyes are love.

I hear her name, Josephine; Josephine Brown, but she is affectionately called Joey.

After my shower, I quickly get dressed in my pajamas, an old T-shirt, and a pair of shorts. I sit down to write at the dining table.

"Tommy," I said, this time auditable.

I wait for him to appear.

Who was the older man?

*They were wearing night clothes, August,* He says. *He must be her husband or lover.*

*Husband,* I said.

Her night clothes don't seem like the kind of apparel one wears if she is just a lover. Her nightgown is the apparel of a bride.

*A bride?* I questioned myself, shocked with my concept.

This young girl is married to the older man.

*Who is the younger Italian?* I think hard.

I try to find some kind of clarity in my thoughts. He looks at Joey as if he is watching over her, like a brother. He is her brother. I hear his name: Donatello, Joey, and his friends call him Donnie. There is a sweet innocent look in her eyes whenever she looks at him, especially when she wants something. I chuckled and thought of Joy and my brother. All she has to do is smile, and my Xavier is putty. She has him wrapped around her finger. He smiles at her and pretty much gives her his whole wallet. Dare I say no, my brother gives me the blues. With Joey and Donnie, he is her big brother, and she is his little sister.

I begin to see the union. Joey is an orphan who is taken in by an Italian widower name Angelo. Angelo, a kind and gentle-natured man. He is giving and always wants to give his last to anyone in need when he is in more need than others. His wife Maria died giving birth to their only son, Donatello. As an adult, Donatello works on the docks in the neighborhood. He takes care of his father, who is ailing.

One particular day, on a Saturday afternoon, Donatello gets home from work. He had brought home dinner. All he wants to do is relax and watch the football game. However, the afternoon is soon turned upside down, changing the lives of Angelo and Donatello forever.

I am in the scene.

Donatello comes home. He and his father talk about trivial matters, from the weather to local neighborhood gossip, but they are interrupted by a loud curdling scream outside the window. Donatello and Angelo quickly run to the window to see what the commotion is and before their eyes is a black man being burned alive and a little girl watching in horror.

*Is that Joey,* I ask.

Joey's father is being lynched.

*Lynch!* I exclaim.

Standing over him is a man in a suit,

*The mob?!*

I look at Tommy,

*I don't know anything about the mob!* I exclaim.

*August, just write.* He urges with intensity.

I am suddenly breathless. I gasped for breath. I ran to the window, the window in my story. I am horrified by the sight. The man, his body burning, his skin burning. His scream sends a chill through my body. He is crying, whaling, calling on Jesus. The Mob Men hold the little girl back as she screams and cries. I look for someone to help her. Someone is going to come to their rescue, but I see no one.

Tommy approaches me and puts his arms around me.

Give me a voice, I cry out to Tommy.

No one can hear me. As the writer, I can voice my opinion, I can express my concerns, but the characters will do what they want, and right now, at this moment, there are no characters to help, no characters to save this man who is burning alive in front of his daughter. There is no one to stop the bad man from his wrath. Although I am in my suite, I sit in my imagination, in my mind, looking from an imaginary window crying hysterically.

*August, shhh,* Tommy tries to me.

I can't stop crying. This poor little girl, this poor man. Why is there no one helping them? Who are these people causing such pain? I fell to my knees and sobbed. I cry as I watch the murder of this man. I cry for the little girl that no one helps. I cry; I cry hard. I can't remember crying this hard. At this moment, I can't imagine how foolish I look in my suite with me on the floor crying, but the images around me are not sofas, chairs, or coffee tables in my suite, but the image of the window and all I hear are the whales and cries of this girl and her father. I don't see the luxurious items in my suite, but I see the child and the burning man crying. I cry hysterically. I am beyond consolable.

**HE IS DEAD. HE** died in front of the little girl's eyes.

*August,* Tommy says my name in a monotone voice.

I sit still on the floor of the suite in shock at the images I saw, the images that I created.

*August,* He says my name again.

Tommy holds me in his arms. He holds me until I manage to regain my composer, bringing me back to my reality. Together we sit on the floor. I leaned my head back and rested my head on his chest.

*It's okay,* he soothes in a soft voice.

I sit up and shake my head. Tommy breaks from his embrace. He shifts his body to face me. His eyes are stern and intense. Tears fall from my eyes.

*Get into the scene,* he said. *And don't let them see you coming.*

I wipe my tears away. I get up off the floor and return to the dining room table. My laptop sits with my thoughts, waiting for me to return.

**THE MOBS LEAVES THE** girl alone on the street. Still sobbing, she fell to her knees sobbing, and still, no one came to her aid. Soon, Donatello watches as his father quickly leaves the apartment. Within moments, nearly seconds, Donatello sees his father on the street with the little girl.

"Pop," Donatello calls out, "What are you doing?"

Angelo, an old feeble Italian man that barely speaks English, is on the street at the scene of the ignored crime. What if they come back and kill him?

"Pop!" Donatello calls out.

Donatello runs after his father. When he gets outside, he sees Angelo grabbing the little girl in his arms and carries her away, carrying her into his building.

"Pop," he says. "What are you doing?"

Angelo pushes him out the way. He doesn't answer him. For an old man, he moves quickly from his son and carrying the child into the apartment. Donatello follows him. He shut and locked the door.

"Pop, take her out of here," Donatello says.

Angelo sits down on the old chair and rocks the girl in his arms as she cries silently in his arms.

"She my baby now," he said sternly.

"No," Donatello exclaimed. "Did you see what happened! This is dangerous! Call the police so they can put her in a home."

"I put her in home, my home," He said.

Angelo continues to coddle her.

"I take care of you, baby." He whispers softly to her.

Nervously, Donatello paces the room, occasionally glancing out of the window with hopes that someone comes looking for her. Still, no signs of anyone coming to see the commotion and the man's body still lies dead on the sidewalk. Donatello looks at his father, rocking the girl. He knows that only the hand of God will change his father's mind to the task that he just volunteered for. Angelo hates to see anyone in need. But considering the danger behind the circumstances, Donatello knows that he had to convince his father that this girl cannot stay here.

"Pop, please," Donatello pleads.

The loud knock on the door startles the three.

"Wat chu doin in dar wit dat chil," asks a voice.

"You go!" Angelo yells

The voice belonged to Ms. Tracy, Donatello, and Angelo's neighbor. She lives across the hall. Ms. Tracy is a very large black woman. She has pretty in the face, but her bombastic nature can be intimidating to most if one doesn't really know her. Angelo and Tracy had a love-hate relationship. She can be an overbearing neighbor, yet in the time of need, she is there for them ever since Donatello was a baby. When Donatello was born, Tracy forced her way into Angelo and Donatello's life.

"Wat you do wit dat baby," she asked Angelo.

Donatello was only a week old. She forced herself into the apartment and saw this man holding the crying baby. She saw the confusion in his eyes. She stood with her hands over her hips shaking her head at Angelo.

"You know nuffin' bout raising baby. Give me baby!"

"Let me be," Angelo yells at her. "My Maria is gone."

Tracy saw the tears in his eyes. He had been crying. His wife had died in childbirth. She reached her hands out to Angelo and took the baby from his arms. Angelo allows Tracy to hold his baby.

"I help ya," Tracy said. "I help you raise baby,"

The baby stopped crying. As he nodded his head, tears fell from Angelo's eyes.

For the next twenty-five years, Tracy was a type of mother to Donatella. Ms. Tracy, as he called her. She scolded him when he was wrong and fed him when he was hungry. After some years, Angelo found comfort in Ms. Tracy's company. Every Friday Angelo would go to her home to fry catfish and enjoy her bosom at night.

Twenty-five years later, Ms. Tracy bangs loudly on the door,

Donatello answers the door.

"I'm trying to get him to call the police," Donatello says as Tracy storms in.

"Hush," Ms. Tracy snaps at Donatello, "Plise don't care bout black chile! No one care bout a child. You see em' coming?"

Donatello sighs.

"She my baby," Angelo expresses.

"You don't get all da babies!" Tracy yells. "You know nuffin' bout raising girl, she a woman girl!"

"Ms. Tracy, what's a woman girl?" Donatello asks

He rubs his temples with frustration. Some of the things that Ms. Tracy says makes no sense. Ms. Tracy looks at Donatello as if he is stupid.

"She teenager old enough for womanhood, but still a girl. I take care of her."

"No!" Angelo yells.

Ms. Tracy pouts. She folds her arms across her chest and slowly paces the room.

"You talk ta him," she said to Donatello.

"He won't listen to me," he said to her. "I am telling him to call the police, social services,"

Ms. Tracy shakes her head.

"No, no," she says. "they no help she not a baby. They toss her aside," Ms. Tracy sits down next to Angelo, "We take her, okay,"

Angelo nods his head with a smile. Ms. Tracy smiles back. She leans in and kisses the girl on the top of her head. Donatello sighs.

I think of Joy. What if some things takes me away from Joy. Would there be one to take her in and immediately consider her as their own? Xavier is a big help with Joy. He forgets that I am her parent and not him, but I have to appreciate the support I get from him.

Donatello is not pleased with the decision that Angelo made with regards to Josephine. It's as if he is tossed aside. Angelo made Donatello give up his bedroom so that she can have it. There have been many sleepless nights that Josephine wakes up screaming. Angelo would comfort her, hold her until she falls asleep. Both Ms. Tracy and Angelo got Josephine in school, and she seems to be doing well. Adjusting was not too difficult for her, but what was strange was that no one came looking for her.

Angelo loves her, loved as his child. Whenever she is with him, he introduces her as his baby. And the love that he gives her, she gives back to him.

Donatello's friends find it comical at the new family dynamic. One particular day, with hopes to enjoy a night of beer, pizza, Donatello and his friend rally at their favorite bar and grill, called Johnny's.

"So how is the little sister thing working out,"

"She's not my sister," Donatello said, rolling his eyes.

"You father is practically calling her his child, which makes her-,"

"An addition," Donatello replied.

They shake their heads and laugh. Donatello sighs.

"Donnie, you have an awkward life. You have a black stepmother-,"

"She's not my stepmother," Donatello snaps. "She's just a friend of the family,"

"She has been like a mother to you, and your father has nights with her," they laugh but not in an insensitive way.

"She seems nice," One of the friends said, named Patrick, a red-headed light-hearted individual.

Donatello shrugs his shoulders.

"Anyway, you know how Pop is; he loves her. That's his baby."

"Is she okay," Patrick asks. "I mean-,"

Donatello sips his beer and the lets out a sigh.

"She's good," Donatello shrugs his shoulders. "As long as Pop loves, I will be there for her. What happened was scary."

His friends nod their heads in agreement.

"Where is she?" Frankie asks.

"She is with Pop, I assume," Donatello answered.

"Let's shoot some pool," they suggested.

For the next few hours, Donatello enjoys the company of his friends. He laughs at their jokes. Music plays in the, and a few of the customers danced on the floor, boyfriends and girlfriends dance on the dance floor. Husbands danced with their wives. Donatello notices a particular couple dancing. They seemed young, too young, and the way they danced seemed too seductive for a local diner. He couldn't see the girl's face because the guy's back is in front of Donatello, and when they turned around, the girl's back is in front of Donatello.

"Don, come, it's your shot," one said, referring to the pool game.

Donatello tries to shoot at the ball with his cue stick, he misses the shot. He sips his beer and casually looks at the couple on the floor.

"They need a room, huh?" one of his friends said.

"At least someone is getting lucky," another friend jokes.

"Get a room!" someone shouts at them.

The comment distracts the couple; they look up from the remarks. The girl's profile is now visible. It is Josephine. Quickly, Donatello walks to the couple.

"Donnie!" Patrick yells.

Donatello ignores him and immediately breaks up the embrace of the couple.

"Hey, man!" the guy exclaims.

"What are you doing?" Donatello said to Josephine.

"She's with me," the kid said.

Donatello looks at the kid.

"If you know what is best for you, you will back up!" he snares.

"You're embarrassing me," Joey exclaims to Donatello.

"Joey, who is this?" the kid asks.

"Don," Donatello's friends calls out as they approach him.

"He's my brother," she says.

"Let's go," Donatello grabs Josephine by the arms.

"You're brother-," her date asks, confused.

Donatello pulls Josephine out of Dave's. He basically drags her to his car and made her get into the car. He drives home.

Inside the house, he slams the door shut and orders her to sit down. Josephine sits on the couch.

"Who's that kid?" Donatello questions

Josephine sits with her arms folded across her chest and gives Donatello a scornful look.

"Donnie, leave me alone," she snaps.

He almost slaps her, but he catches himself.

"What was the kid doing?" Donatello asks. "You were supposed to be with Pop."

"Pop went to Miss. Tracy's and I called some friends to meet me at Johnny's."

"What were you doing with that kid?" Donatello interrogates.

"Dancing!"

"That looked more like dancing!" he accuses.

"So,"

"So, Josephine, you're only thirteen years old."

"He said that he like me,"

"Just because a guy likes you don't mean you get fresh with him," Donatello said to her.

"Then what if he doesn't like me anymore,"

"Then he's a bum!"

"Why you care? You don't speak to me anyway!"

"Because Pop loves you, and he believes you are out being a good girl!"

"I am a good girl; I was just dancing!" Josephine defends.

"If you're such a good girl, you be here instead of out acting like some tramp."

Josephine looks away. She starts crying. Donatello begins to feel sorry for yelling her. She has been through so much. Is she lashing out? He sits down beside to her.

"I'm sorry," Donatello said softly. "It's just the circumstances of you being here makes me nervous, and I don't want Pop getting hurt."

Josephine wipes her tears away.

"You coming here did turn some things around, but Pop, he is crazy about you. You're his baby, and I have to protect you from him."

Josephine doesn't reply.

"Why do you think no one has come for you?" Donatello asks.

"Cuz it just was just me and my daddy." Josephine said. "My mama died when I was a baby. I ain't got no one else, 'cept you, Pop and Ms. Tracy."

Donatello takes in a deep breath. He looks at Josephine. For the first time, he saw her as that frail, helpless little girl that was screaming outside his window a few months ago. He saw that sweet innocent child and felt sorry for her. There is no one? At least Donatello has his father, and thankfully Miss. Tracy. His mind recalls when Josephine referred to him as her brother. He recalls that there was no hesitation in her eyes or her voice when she told that kid that Donatello is her brother.

"You called me your brother," Donatello said with a smirk.

"I didn't know what else to call you," Josephine said.

Donatello nods his head, accepting the title as the brother. Considering he is the only child, the idea of him being a brother is strange. He looks on his friends as types of extended family, even Miss. Tracy is a type of parent to him. Together Josephine and Donatello look at each other. Donatello's mind, he has this young girl that is sharing his home, his father, and now his pseudo-mother. Is she his sister? He grins at her. She smiles back. Yes, she will be his little sister. Who else will care for her the way his father has and Miss Tracy?

"I'll be your brother, and you be my sister," Donatello said.

From that moment on, Donatello and Josephine build a bond. He became the overprotective brother, and she is his little sister. He made sure that she stayed out of trouble, made sure that no one bothered her. Donatello made sure that she maintained good grades in school. The kid at Johnny's, Willie, almost feared Donatello. He actually liked Josephine and promised to treat her like a lady. But Donatello told him that his sister is not dating until she was eighteen.

*Tommy, I don't see that older guy,* I said.

Just keep writing, he coaxes.

*I am getting tired. I don't have any energy to write anymore. But I want to know who that older guy is.* I look at Tommy.

*It's okay to rest,* Tommy says with a chuckle.

But the last two books, I wrote in one night. And this book, I can tell that I had not gotten anywhere close to the scene that I saw when I was at Darnell's.

*That's because you're tired.*

I look at the clock and see that it is only two am.

I am so angry. It seems like I have written for hours. I look at my notes; it looks like I have written for a few hours. I feel defeated. Reluctantly I walk to the bed and lay down. I turn on on my side and see Tommy lying beside me.

*What's the matter?* He asks.

*Why are you still here if I can't write anymore?* I ask.

*Because the story is still in you,* he said, pointing to his head. *It's just that you are physically tired.*

I close my eyes and go to sleep.


**I DON'T WASTE TIME** getting dressed. I didn't wait for a wake-up call from the front desk. By the time they called, I already showered and dressed. I want to get back to my book and to see who that older guy is. As I look over my notes, I get my morning call from Joy; she told me about her adventures in Pixburgh.

"Pittsburgh," I corrected.

Why can't she get that right? I ask myself.

"Uncle X took me to Kennywood. I had a funnel cake, ice cream dots, I got on the rides, and Uncle X got me a big teddy bear with a Kennywood shirt."

"Sounds like you having a ball," I said, smiling.

"Mom, I want to come here every summer, okay," she told me.

"Sure, Joy," I said.

"Mommy, Uncle X, and I saw a lady reading one of your books."

"Did you," I asked.

"Yeah," she said.

I could tell that she was smiling. I heard crunching sounds in my ear.

"Joy, what are you eating?"

"Cereal," she answered. "Uncle Benny gave me some cereal,"

Uncle Benny is one of my father's brothers. X. and Joy were staying with our Uncle Benny during their stay. Uncle Benny is also another relative that caters to Joy.

"Joy, where is X.," I ask.

"He's in the shower," Joy answers crunching her cereal.

"Is there milk in that cereal?" I ask, sitting up.

"No," she said. "Uncle Benny gave me some Cookie Crisp."

I could hear her contentment. As she crunched her Cookie Crisp, I could see her sitting on one of Uncle Benny's modern-day, upscale couches, swinging her legs, shoving a handful of cookie balls in her mouth, bobbing her head from side to side, happy, full of joy.

"Your uncle is going to get you for eating dry cereal," I stated.

For a brief moment, I hoped Xavier would get on Joy for eating dry cereal, and he sees that she really enjoys dry cereal.

"No," she said in a carefree way.

Of course not; my brother gives Joy everything.

"Mom, let me tell you about the lady," she said. "Okay, she was reading your book, and I said, 'My mom wrote that book,' and she looks at me and smiles. Then Uncle X smiled at her and said that he's your brother and I am your daughter. The lady asks my name; I said, 'Joy Banks,' She shook Uncle X's hand and said that she loves your work. Mommy, someone loves you!"

Joy was so excited. I couldn't help but laugh at her excitement.

"Then me and Uncle X went to the bookstores, and we saw your name on a big poster and your books on the shelves. So, when you come here, I will show you, okay?"

"Okay, Joy," I said, smiling.

There was a knock at my door.

"Joy, I gotta go."

"Okay, Mommy, I love you."

"I love you too, Joy,"

I answer the door. Entering in with a smile, my dry cleaning and my large hazelnut latte is my faithful assistant.

"You look rested, August," she said to me.

"Really," I asked.

I take a quick look in the mirror.

"I just went to bed at two," I told her.

She shakes her head and laughs.

"I don't know how you do it," she replied. "We need to get packed and checked out before your book signing at ten. Everything is already set up in Dallas. Plus, I managed to get you an interview with Miles Palmer; he is coming to Dallas."

"You got him coming to Dallas?" I ask.

She nods her head.

"Why?" I ask.

"What do you mean why?" she asked. "He's been trying to get an interview with you since the beginning of the month."

"I know, but I don't want to interview with him," I state.

"Why?" she asks.

Before I can answer, my cell phone rings. I look at the screen and see that it is Adam.

"Hello," I answer the phone.

"Good morning," Adam says cheerfully.

"Hi, Adam. Maya and I are getting ready to head to Dallas." I inform.

As I talked to Adam on the phone, Maya and I went to the lounge to get breakfast.

"Good," Adam comments. "I read *The Beautiful Ones*; I loved it."

"Adam, I don't like it," I said.

"What you mean you don't like it, you wrote it." He questioned.

"The characters, I don't like them," I said to him.

Maya and I head to the far corner of the lounge. As she set the laptop for me, Adam fusses at me, I mouthed the words; thank you, to Maya and watched her rush off to the buffet table.

"You don't like them," he asked as if I am being petty.

"They are shallow, malicious, shrewd, and what was strange I was comfortable writing it,"

"What?" Tommy ask.

I can tell that he is confused.

"Adam, that book makes me nervous."

"August, this book is everything that you think you need. You want that Gatsby? Well, it's in this book,"

"I don't want my Gatsby to be dirty,"

"What do you think Gatsby is, just a heck of a nice guy! Why am I arguing with you?"

"I am working on something else," I informed.

"I don't want to hear it, I'll talk to you when you get back," he hung up the phone on me.

Maya returns to the table with her plate full of food.

"You're not eating?" she asked.

"Yeah, in a minute," I said.

"Is everything all right with Adam?" she asks.

I sigh then shrug my shoulders,

"Who knows, he is so temperamental," I reply.

"What's the problem?" she asks.

"Who knows,"

I begin to look over my notes, I look at the character development of Josephine. Is she like The Beautiful Ones? Josephine is beautiful, brown skin the color of an almond, big dark brown colored eyes, those eyes spoke volumes to Donatello. He truly loves her, he wants to protect her. He didn't understand at first how connected his father and Ms. Tracy were to this child. Donatello wondered why his heart was not as touched as his father's. Now, Donatello cannot imagine life without her. Josephine makes him happy. His friends, Alfred, Frankie, and Patrick, respected the relationship of Donatello and Josephine, they were commissioned to protect and watch Josephine when Donnie wasn't around. The Boys, who became types of brothers to Josephine made sure that she stayed out of trouble. They made sure that she did what she was supposed to do. Josephine did didn't go anywhere without the protection of The Boys. Whenever Donatello wasn't around, they made sure she went straight home from school, didn't get into any trouble. With them, she was never alone. Donatello or They Boys were always somewhere around, not far.

"AUGUST!" MAYA CALLS MY name, bringing me from The Land of Aug.

I look up from my notes,

"I have a few phone calls to make with your travel. I'll be right back."

I nodded my head. I watch her leave. Within moments, I see Tommy walking to the table. He sits down where Maya sat.

*Are you ready?* He asks.

I nod my head.

*Let's go*

Four years have gone by, Josephine is seventeen years old works after school, part-time as a waitress at a local jazz club, by Willie's father, whom she affectionately Mr. William. The jazz club is called Billie's, which was a play on the legendary Billie Holiday and the nickname to William. To keep an eye on Josephine and to earn little extra money, Donatello and his friends also worked at Billie's. Alfred did the accounting; he helped Mr. William balance his books. Patrick served as a waiter, Frankie supplied the muscle, and Donnie alongside Willie worked as bartenders. Donatello kept a close eye on the bums that would try to flirt or hit on Joey.

"I don't need a babysitter," she says to him one night over dinner.

He doesn't verbally reply. He looks at her with eyes indicating that she is not getting rid of him. He returns to his meal.

"How did you do on that English paper?"

"Okay," she said with a casual shrug.

"What's okay?" he questions.

"I got a 'B,'" she answers.

Donnie nods his head, accepting the B.

"Donnie, don't talk to me as if you didn't hear what I said. I don't need a baby sister. You scowling at my tables at work is keeping me from doing well and making the good tips."

"Joey, some of those men that come to your table-,"

"Are being them," Josephine said. "They know better to ask me out on a date before coming to you."

120

Donatello chuckles at Josephine's comment.

If any guy considered dating Joey, the advice given is:

"That's Donatello's sister, talk to him first,"

Josephine hated Donatello's overprotected barrier, especially when it came to dating because she knew that Donatello knew that she didn't want to date just anyone, she had her eyes set on Willie. And this pleased Willie because of his feelings for Josephine, but Donatello made sure that she belonged to no one until she finished high school.

Donatello looks at his sister. She looks at him with intensity in her eyes.

"Don't look at me like that," he said. "I'm protecting you."

"I appreciate that, but I don't need that kind of protection. It's intimidating and embarrassing. Trust me enough to make the right decisions and to handle myself."

Donatello sits back in his seat, surrendering to his sister.

"I've been living here for four years. You, Pop, and Ms. Tracy have made me feel safe than I ever have."


"You're real good with her," William said to Donatello.

Saturday night, during closing William watches as Donatello keeps one on Josephine and the other on washing the counter. Donatello grins at William's comment.

"Most girls her age are chasing boys not focused on school. Considering what she been through, she is happy."

"I've been told that I am too controlling with her," Donatello says.

William hands him a beer. From behind the bar, William and Donatello watch as Josephine and the other servers clean their tables. She laughs at Patrick playfully teased her.

"No one came looking for the girl?" William asks.

Donnie shakes his head and sips his beer.

"Still," William questions.

Donatello shakes his head.

"Does she talk about it?" William asks.

Donatello shakes his head no.

"She used to have nightmares, but for the past few years she has been okay."

William nods her head.

*August, there he is,* Tommy whispered. *Write?*

One particular night at Billie's unexpected guest enters. His apparel speaks of money; he wears an Armani suit. His presence stirs up nervous and anxious actions because he is not the type of man that would venture out to a jazz club especially in this part of town, but tonight he is here at Billie's. His name is Beau Coltogirone. His reputation is not worthy of note. He is ruthless gangster, a mobster, a killer, and his presence is beyond intimidating because no one knew why he is on the scene.

"Gentlemen," William says to Coltogirone, and his entourage. "What can I do for you?"

Coltogirone grins,

"I hear that this little place is quite nice. We came to see why,"

William hesitates in offering him a seat.

"We don't want any trouble," Coltogirone says to him. "Just to enjoy good music and good food."

Coltogirone extends his hand to Mr. William. Mr. William grins and shakes his hand. The live band continues to play jazz as the hostess escorts Coltogirone and his entourage to an empty table- in Josephine's section.

*What is going on,* I ask myself.

The lights in the hotel lounge suddenly become dim. Suddenly, I am no longer in the hotel lounge but at Billie's. I see everyone, William, Donatello, Josephine, The Boys. I close my eyes and watch as Josephine slowly walks to the bar where Donatello and Willie are working. Soon William, The Boys, and a young waitress quickly approach the bar.

"I can take Joey's table," the young waitress offers.

Donatello nods his head, but Josephine declines.

"I want the table," Josephine protests.

"Joey," Donatello admonishes.

"It's okay," Joey says looking at him. "I'll be okay,"

Everyone knows that if Donatello made a scene, he could erupt whatever scheme Coltogirone is planning. However, Donatello is not about to let his sister serve Coltogirone. William walks to Cologirone's table to assure him that someone will be with him shortly. Donatello tries to convince Josephine not to take the table.

William returns back to the bar.

"Give someone else the table," Donatello says to William.

"Donnie, I will be fine," Josephine says sternly looking at Donatello and William.

William has to think fast. He doesn't want anyone to get hurt especially if Coltogirone is here for the negative. Quickly William glances at the crowd. Although the music that the band is playing is lively, the tension is thick. Some of the staff are carrying guns.

"How many tables do you have Patty?" William asks.

"William, his section is slammed," Josephine expresses. "Plus, it is my table."

"Joey, your brother-," William begins.

"Forget him," she snaps, interrupting Mr. William.

She looks at Donatello.

"I'll be okay,"

Quickly, Josephine grabs her tray and walks to her table.

"Good evening, I am Joey," Josephine says smiling. "I will be your girl tonight. What can I start you boys off with tonight?"

Donatello watches as his sister entertain and serve Beau Coltogirone and his entourage.

"Don, calm down," William said. "She's okay."

Throughout the evening, Josephine serves Beau and his group. She uses her charm to entertain them.

Josephine flirts playfully making them smile and laugh. Coltogirone is mesmerized by Josephine. She has the sweetest smile; her eyes dance every time she laughs.

"Your boyfriend has been watching," Coltogione says to her glancing at Donatello.

"That's not my boyfriend," she said with a grin. "He's my brother,"

"You're brother?" Coltogione asked with a chuckle.

"Yes, I'm adopted." She answered.

Coltogione nodded his head.

"He's very overprotective of me,"

"Oh yeah why is that?" asked one of the members of Coltogione's entourage.

"Because I'm his little sister, all big brothers look after their little sisters. Do you have any sisters, Mr. Beau?"

"Yeah," he answered. "I am the youngest in the family. My big sisters mother me. But tell your brother to relax, I like you. How old are you,"

"I'll be eighteen in May," she answers.

His eyes look over Josephine's body. Her eyes approved of his intrigue.

*August, are you serious? He asked me. Why does she like him?*

I smile. He doesn't see it coming.

**"AUGUST!" I JUMP, STARTED** out of my seat.

I look up, and it is Maya standing before me. The scenery has changed. I am back in the hotel lounge no longer at Billie's. I take in a deep breath and then sigh.

"We gotta go," Maya says.

I look at my watch, and it is almost nine am.

Seriously where did the time go?

I am not in the mood for a book signing. I need to write. Why did Beau Coltgirone sit in Joey's section? I know that Donatello wants to flip or will he. Can he keep his cool? I can cancel this book signing, go back into my seat and go back to Billie's to see what will happen, but I can't let my fans down, and Adam will kill me. This book is Gatsby because I can feel the intensity. I see the green light of hope as Donatello tries to provide a stable environment for Josephine. Their family is not the traditional family, but they're family. The dream is obtainable because despite Josephine start, she is living the life that would be unattainable to others. As I think of Donatello watching from the bar as his sister serves and entertains Beau Coltgirone, I can feel Donatello's blood boiling. He can't do anything but just sit on stand-by because no one wants to disturb the beast in Coltigrone.

I am going to press through these next couple of hours. Once I am on the plane, I can focus on what is important- creating my Gatsby.

## 4

His dark eyes are sinister; there is no life in them. When you see him, there is death, he has no soul. However, whenever he looks into her eyes, he smiles. There seems to be something magical about her. She soothes him. She calms the beast that lived within him. To him, she is fascinating. Every Friday, Coltogirone would come and bring his entourage and sit in her section. It is impressive and strange to watch how cool and calm she is around him. One night Donatello asked her about her mannerisms dealing with Beau Coltogirone

"Why are you playing with him?"

"I'm not playing with him," Josephine says.

"Joey, that man is dangerous! Don't play his game,"

Josephine listens to his warnings, but she wants Coltogirone, she wants him.

I stop writing.
*August, don't stop Tommy pleads.*
I continue to write.

Josephine's eighteenth birthday. Donatello hosted her birthday party at Billie's. William had closed the club down, and friends and family have come to celebrate her. Donatello has put a lot of time and money into making this the best birthday for his little sister. He sits back and smiles as she dances with her friends and family. Speaking of friends, Willie secretly has a bracelet for Josephine. He had worked long hours to make extra money to get her the gift. He plans on giving it to her in private, alone in a park. He's going to tell her that he loves her, and now that she is eighteen, she can be his girl and Donnie can't stop it.

During the party, an unexpected and uninvited visitor arrives.

*Beau Coltogirone!* I exclaim.

He comes in with his entourage.

"Mr. Coltogirone," William said. "We're closed today,"

"Yes, I know," Coltogirone said. "I am here to see Josephine."

He smiles in Josephine's direction.

"She invited me,"

Shocked and stunned; everyone gasps at this fact. William grins, quickly he glances at Josephine. She smiles at Coltogirone. William smiles at Coltogirone and says:

"Well then, help yourself to the food, and enjoy."

"Thank you,"

As the music resumes and Coltogirone and his entourage take their seats, Donatello quickly grabs Josephine by the arm and takes her into the back room. For a long moment, he looks at her ready to kill her. She looks at him with her big doe eyes.

"He asked me if I had plans for my birthday," she speaks first.

"How does he know when your birthday is?" Donatello questions.

"He asked,"

Donatello signs and paces the floor.

"Donnie, what was I supposed to do? Tell him to mind his business? He kill us both."

"You playing with fire little girl," Donatello warns.

"I'm trying to keep the peace," she said. "I can't be rude,"

"No, but you're acting as if you like him." He says.

Josephine doesn't reply, she looks away.

"Joey-,"

She looks up at him.

"I know how to handle him," she says.

"Joey-," Donatello admonishes.

"Donnie, I'm not afraid of him." She says. "You don't have to worry about me," she says as she put her arms around him.

Donatello looks somber. She stands on her tippy toe and gives him an Eskimo kiss.

"It's my birthday," she says. "Please be nice."

Donatello sighs then kiss Josephine on the forehead.

"How do you manage to have me and Pop wrapped around your finger?"

She giggles hugging him, and then together they walk back to the party. Patrick, Frankie, Alfred, and Willie all look at Donatello, he nods his head to indicate that all is well.

**I LOOK UP AND** see Miles Palmer standing in before me. I am in Dallas. I've been in Dallas for two days. Everything is a fog for me because even though I remember seeing the fans at the book signings and I remember signing their books, and I remember doing interviews with local newspapers, my mind has been in my work. Now, I am sitting in a local diner eating a turkey sandwich with provolone cheese.

Maya had reminded me of my interview with Miles Palmer, but as mentioned, my mind was a fog. I was very adamant of not wanting to interview him. However, my pretty and stylish assistant pushed me to face my fears and meet with the King of Literature Critic. So here I sit in a small diner in Dallas.

"Hi, August," he says to me smiling.

"Hi," I replied, staring directly into his blue eyes.

As he sits down, a waitress approaches the table.

"What can I get for you," she asks.

"A cheeseburger, well done," he said to her, "With a coke,"

She nods her head and then walks away. I watched Miles as he got himself organized. He pulls out a digital recorder, a small notebook, and then he pulls out a copy of my book. To my surprise, it looks worn out. My book is not that old to look tattered.

"Were you working on a new book?" he asks.

"Yes,"

He grins.

"Well thank you for granting me this interview, I know that you're busy."

"You're welcome," I said managing to break awa

"First of all, I am a big fan, I mean big fan. Your work is old school with new school characters. Characters that we can see today, but they're old school, yet current enough for us to relate to them." He tapped the copy of my book. "What was your motivation because I didn't see it coming."

"You didn't?"

"No," Miles says smiling.

He has a nice smile.

"I felt the emotion, the pain, you know, but when you actually thought that it was it-BOOM!" he exclaims.

The waitress returns with Miles' coke.

"Your burger will be here in a minute,"

Miles nods his head, and she walks away. He sips his drink then looks at me as if he is waiting for an answer.

"What?" I ask.

"What was your motivation?"

"Oh," I thought replied. "Ah, I don't know, I just saw something and wrote it."

"What writers inspire you?"

"Fitzgerald," I answered quickly.

"Really?"

"Yes, *The Great Gatsby* is my favorite book."

"That is a great book," Miles said smiling, nodding. "One of my favorites."

I could not imagine this beautiful man a fan of Fitzgerald's.

"August tell me, your last book you dedicated to Tommy Gibbs, the actor right?"

"Yes,"

"What is the connection? He's an actor, you're a writer. Nothing in your work reflects him- what is the connection?"

"There isn't one," I answer.

"You two good friends?"

"Never met him," I answer.

Miles look at me puzzled.

My subconscious is my little secret. With X. always putting me in the Land of Aug, and this beautiful man with the power to put me in the bottom of the barrel when it comes to literature.

*Don't' let them see you coming,* said a familiar voice in my ear.

I am surprised to hear him at this moment because I am not writing. The waitress comes back with Miles' cheeseburger. I watch as he blesses his food and then quickly takes a bit out of his cheeseburger.

"You're from Pittsburgh?" he asks.

"Yes, I moved to New York when my daughter was five,"

"How old is she now?"

"She's ten," I answer.

"So besides writing best sellers and spending time with your daughter, what is a day like for August Schofield."

"That's it," I answer. "I live a boring life. I love to write. I'm always writing."

"Were you working on something new?" Miles ask.

I nodded my head.

"What?" he asks with a curious grin.

"You'll see," I answer, being coy.

He chuckles then sips his coke.

"Are you enjoying the tour?"

"It's been entertaining," I say with a chuckle.

"Oh, how so?"

I think about the dinner I had with Literary Royalty, there were The Beautiful Ones, and now I am staring at a man that is too beautiful to be real. Oh, and there are creative hallucinations.

Miles sipped his soda and waited for an answer.

"It's been fun," I say with a grin.

"A writer with little words," he comments, then takes a bit out of his hamburger.

I look out the window wondering if I should elaborate more, but to be truthful, I don't really remember anything about the book tour because I am mainly writing.

"This current book, what was your motivation,"

Again, I think about my answer. How do I say, I am motivated by my illusions of Tommy Gibbs. He advises me not to let them see it coming.

"My motivation for this book came from the song *November Rain*,"

Miles is shocked. I watch him go through his book. It is dog-eared and has post-it notes throughout the pages. He looks at me with a grin and then shakes his head.

"I would have never guessed that." He says.

I grin.

"Would you mind if I ask you a few questions about the book?" he asks.

"Sure,"

Miles looks at me. Here it comes. This is what makes Miles Palmer ruthless. He questions about the concepts of a writer's work. I sit up in my chair ready to answer or not answer any question that he throws out.

"You seem nervous," he comments.

"I am interviewing Miles Palmer," I state.

"You don't have to be nervous. I won't ask you anything crazy,"

I respond by taking a deep breath. Miles grin and sips his drink.

"Well, I can see that you're bit stand-offish, you really didn't answer my questions, so I think I need to take a different approach."

"I've answered your questions," I said with a chuckle.

"You did?" he asks with doubt.

"Yes,"

"We've been here for almost ten minutes, and the only questions you've answered was that you admire F. Scott Fitzgerald and your daughter. Valued information, but the readers and I want to know you, August Schofield."

"Believe it or not, I am not an interesting person. My best friend is a journal and a good balled point pen. When I am not writing, I am chasing my daughter, or she is chasing me."

"So, the passion of your life are in your characters."

"I suppose,"

"Are your characters and their situations related to you?"

"In some form, but they're not memoirs or biographies. I just enjoy writing. If I think of a story, I tell it."

Miles grins.

"Your work has made people think, such as this book. A marriage on the rocks after thirty plus years. It's like after all this time, after all these years, why not trust love."

"It wasn't that she didn't trust love, she just didn't trust him."

"So why waste his time and hers?"

"That's a good question," I said. "I only wish I could answer it."

I watch him take a bit his cheeseburger and as he chews, wipes his mouth and then licks his lips. At that moment, I wish that I am his cheeseburger. This man is too handsome. He is amazingly gorgeous. He looks at me, his ocean-colored eyes hold me still. I take a deep breath and then slowly exhale.

"The husband in this book, he hoped that maybe his wife would love him," Miles asked.

"No, he hoped that she had forgiven him from how he acted in the past."

"Did she?"

"You read it, you tell me what she saw," I said with a chuckle.

Miles grins at me,

"I saw a woman that was never going to trust him and the fact that he knew that grieved him and that gave her much pleasure."

I look away. My eyes scan the dinner. I look back at Miles.

"Good observation,"

Miles finishes his hamburger just in time for the waitress to come over.

"Can I offer you desert?"

"Do you have any peach cobbler?" he asks.

"Yes," she said with a smile. "Would you like a slice, Ms. Schofield?"

"Sure," I answered. "With coffee please,"

The waitress takes Miles's plate and leaves.

"I'm glad that you like my observation," he says with a grin.

"Why?"

"August, I am a fan. So, if you like what I think about your book, then I am okay."

I grin.

"As a fan, can I ask you a question?"

"Shoot?"

The waitress returns with our cobbler and coffee and then she leaves.

"Tommy Gibbs,"

"What about him?" I asked, eating.

"Why are your books dedicated to him?"

I look out the window again then focus on the cobbler.

"I wish that I could explain the concept of the dedication, but I can't.

"Why?" he asks putting a piece of cobbler into his mouth.

I take a deep breath and then I slowly exhale.

"Because I don't want to," I reply calmly.

I hope that I didn't offend him. I feel silly about my evasiveness.

"I want to explain, but I-," I stammer.

"Don't explain," he said. "A muse comes in all forms."

I look at him as if I am busted. As if he just found out Top Secret Information. I suddenly felt numb, and I am suddenly afraid; why I had no clue. No one knew about Tommy but me. I know people are curious as to why my book is dedicated to him. The fact that he is my muse is mind-boggling because we have nothing in common. There is no real connection. So how did Miles figure it out? I don't want anyone to know. If anyone should know, it should be Tommy. I wouldn't know how to explain why and lately if I would explain how I would be institutionalized.

"What do you think he would say if he were to find out that he is your muse?"

I shrugged my shoulders.

"I don't know, why does it matter?"

"Because I like you," he said. "I admire your work, I want to know who inspires you."

I sip my coffee.

"Put this in your article," I said. "Writing is therapeutic. It's calming and other than my kid, it is the most wonderful gift."

Miles seems to know me, not like a reporter that knew their research but as if he knows the most intimate secrets. I quickly begin to gather up my things, and I summon the waitress over,

"August-," Miles says.

"I have to run," I said.

The waitress comes to the table. I put down a fifty dollar bill on the table and stood up.

"It was nice meeting you," I said then leave.

I don't want anyone to know me that intimately. When it comes to my writing, my thoughts are personal until I am ready to share them. It is as if my mind is a secret journal and he reads me page by page.

**I SIT IN A** bathtub full of bubbles, lavender, and vanilla scented bubbles. I feel my body melting in the hot water. My mind was going over the last hour. When I arrive at my suite, I shut the blinds making sure nothing can creep in, no sunlight-nothing, as if I'm hiding. Why am I suddenly afraid of my own shadow? As I sat in the tub, I kept seeing Miles aquamarine-colored eyes and seeing his cool demeanor searching for hidden secrets, lost valuable treasure. There is no lost treasure, lost marbles maybe but no treasure. Miles wanted to know my connection to Tommy Gibbs. No one will understand if they find out about me and my muse. People will wonder if I like him-they will wonder if it is more than a creative attraction. I don't want him, like that, there are no romantic feelings towards him. It is just the way he makes me think. As if he encourages me to go into the gulf of my imagination and discover the creative possibilities. Stories that people never think about. If my imaginary stimulator can make me do that, then what could Miles do? See all that and try to fathom my concept.

Does God reveal his secrets; of course not. The hymn goes, "And will understand it better, by and by," He lets you in just enough to bask in his glory and goodness. We don't see the face of God, not until that Great Day. But my writing, I don't want them to see my face, just enjoy my works.

The bathtub was soothing. I began to think about Joey and her sick attraction to Coltogirone. No one could understand why, especially Donatello and especially my Tommy. I knew why, but I couldn't reveal the secret. They will understand it better by and by.

*I cannot believe you are leaving me in the dark.* He said.

He was sitting in the tub. His hair is wet and soapy. I got nervous and almost jumped out of the tub.

*August relax,* he said to me. *I'm in here.* He pointed to his head.

You're in my tub! I shouted. Get out of my tub!

*August, I am a figment of your imagination.*

*I don't want to see this side of you, or you see this side of me.*

*You can't see me, not in that way,*

*I see you in my tub.* I replied.

*But you don't see me, nothing personal anyway, I can't see you.* Tommy said.

I looked at him carefully trying to make sure that he wasn't lying about these hallucinations.

*Me and you, -*he began. *There is nothing romantic. But I am where you are, in here. He pointed to his head again.*

I sat back in the tub.

*I'm a sick, sick person.*

*Why?* Tommy ask.

I looked at him bewildered by his why. Why would he wonder why I think that I am sick?

*August, again, I am only here as mental stimulation. Not physical.*

*But why now when I am naked in the tub, and you appear to be also?*

*Because you started brainstorming while you're in the tub, I'm where you are, mentally. You're okay; we're okay.* Tommy said.

I sunk deep into the tub, the bubbles surrounded me.

*What's Joey's interest in with Beau,* Tommy asked.

As I closed my eyes, I began to hear jazz music playing softly in the background.

"Josephine, why baby," Ms. Tracy whispered to her. Josephine didn't answer. "Donatello ain't going to like dis. Oh, he is goin' ta be upset!"

"I'm an adult, Ms. Tracy," Josephine said.

I looked across the bathroom and saw Joey sitting in the bathtub. Ms. Tracy was washing her back.

*Too many people in this bathroom* I thought to myself.

Together, both Josephine and I get out of the tub. We dried ourselves off. It was like a mirror image; we put our robes on then left the bathroom. Tommy was now on the bed; dry and fully dressed. I quickly put on an old pair of sweats and sat down at my laptop and began to write.

The night of Joey's birthday party, Willie never got the chance to take her to a park and profess his love to her.  The way Josephine seemed when she was with Coltogirone during her party, made it clear to Willie that she liked Coltogirone, not him. Still, Coltogirone and his crew would still go to Mr. Williams and sit in Josephine's section, and he would bring her a red rose with each visit. It had been rumored that Joey has been dating Beau Coltogirone.  As hard as they tried to hide, few people would see her with him. At first, Donatello didn't entertain the rumors. But one day, he decided to find out how true they were.

One particular evening, he waited for her to come home. She was accompanied by Frankie, Alfred, and Patrick. Joey was surprised to see Donatello waiting for her.

"Don," Alfred said to him with a grin. "What are you doing here?"

"Where you been?" Donatello asked Josephine.

"Out," she answered, trying to be vague glancing quickly at the boys.

"Out where?" he asked. "And with who?"

He stood up and walked towards her, backing her into a corner. At first, Frankie stood in front of Joey trying to protect her from Donatello's rage. He could see that his friend was going to snap if Joey said the wrong thing. Donatello looked at Frankie. Frankie stepped aside. Not because he was afraid of Donatello, but he knew to step back at this particular moment. Donatello starred Josephine. He looked hard into her eyes trying to read her. Josephine tried hard to look away. He took his finger and lifted her chin so that she could look at him in the eyes.

"I'm hearing rumors, Joey that you're going around town with Beau Coltogirone," Donatello said. She looked away. "Joey, didn't I tell you not to play with him."

"I'm not playing." She said. Josephine managed to slip away from Donatello. She took a deep breath and announced: "We're getting married,"

Immediately filled with rage, Donatello slapped Josephine across the face. She fell to the ground. Stunned, but not shocked, Alfred helped her to her feet. Patrick and Frankie ran over to hold Donatello back.

"I am not a child, Donnie!" she exclaimed.

"Have you lost your mind?!" he shouted.

"No, I know what I am doing!"

Donatello could understand why Joey would marry a villain like Coltogirone. Was he forcing her? Did she feel like she didn't have a choice?

"Joey," Donatello approached her, but she pushed him away, holding the side of her face. She was crying and bleeding from the corner of her lip. "I'm sorry,"

"Joey tells him," Patrick said.

"Tell me what?" Donatello asked.

Alfred gets ice for Joey; he wrapped it up in a cloth and helped apply it to her face. Alfred led Joey to a vacant seat.

Donatello waited for an answer. Everyone glanced at each other.

"Joey," Frankie said.

She nervously looked at him. Then she looked at Donatello, tears were in her eyes.

"Beau Coltogirone killed my parents," she said.

Donatello looked perplexed.

"That day when Pop took me in. It was Coltogirone who killed my father, burned him alive right in front of me. They killed my mother before they kill my dad."

"Does Coltogirone know who you are?" Donatello asked.

"No,"

"Joey, are you sure?"

"Yes, you don't forget a face," she snapped. "Plus, his ring, it was my father's. It has his initials, J.B., that was my father's. Joseph Brown."

"So why are you marrying him?"

"Beef," she said with no emotions. "I'm going to kill him."

"Joey," Donatello said, he kneeled down at her feet, "You can't-,"

Josephine nodded her head.

"He has Allie running his books," Joey said referring to Alfred. "And Frankie and Patty, are his muscles."

Donatello looked at his friends in horror.

"What?" Donatello said stunned.

"We need you to be his right hand," Frankie said.

"No, this is suicide!" Donatello exclaimed. "Joey stop this now,"

She shook her head. "he's going to pay,"

"Baby," Donatello said as he cupped his hands around her face, she flinched slightly cause of the spot where he hit her. Donatello leaned in and kissed the tender area. He then looked her in the eyes. "Whose idea was this?"

"Joey's," Patrick answered.

"Why are you involved?" Donatello stood up to face his friends.

"Because we love Joey," Alfred answered "We love you, and Beau Coltogirone can hurt one of us and get away with it. He's hurt some many people."

"And he trusts you,"

"He trusts Joey, and Joey trusts us," Patrick said. "With you as his right hand, we can get in and take him down."

"We are not a powerful force!" Donatello snapped.

"Donnie please," Josephine stood up with tears fell from her eyes. Donatello saw pain. "He took my life away from me,"

"But me and Pop-,"

"I will always be grateful for you and Pop and Ms. Tracy, but I need closure. What if he does this to another little girl?"

"What if we fail," he said in a soft tone.

"We won't," Josephine said. "We have his trust, through me. Allie will run his books, make sure that in the end, I will collect everything. Patty and Frankie will be his muscle, to prove their loyalty, and you, just be his right hand-,"

"We may have to kill people, Joey," Donatello said.

"No that's the thing, we manage to spare whoever lives. You as his right hand, you can talk to him, make him think he is going crazy. With his trust in you, you pick the doctors. He will get so crazy we make his death look like a suicide."

"Joey," Donatello shook his head. He ran his fingers through his hair.

"Donnie," Patrick said. "It will work,"

"How are you so sure?"

"Because he is putty in her arms," Patrick said.

Donatello sighed. He looked over at Josephine.

I saved my work. Shut down my laptop.

*August, what are you doing?*

*Taking a break.*

*Finish, I want to know what is happening.*

I looked at Tommy. He was intrigued. Will Donatello help Josephine and their friends take down one of the city's most notorious mobster? Because my muse has been good to me, I decided not to torture him. I continued to write well into the night.

**I LAY IN BED** not wanting to get up. But I knew that I would have to soon because Joy would charge into my room ready for camp that I decided to put her in for the rest of the summer. There she can make macaroni necklaces, go swimming, and chase other kids around and they can chase her. I was home from my book tour. For the past six weeks, I have done nothing but just lounge around my house, watching meaningless soap operas, watch TV Land and read books. My book that I went on tour for is now in its second printing, and it is only a few months old. Per Adam, I had a successful tour. I don't remember much of it. Not that I blacked out or lost consciousness, I just don't really remember too much about the tour. I remember going to several bookstores to meet and greet my fans. I remember signing their books,

*Thank you for your support,*
*Love August Schofield*

I remember going to the various talk shows. Chatting and laughing with the celebrity host and hostess and then telling the audience:

"Everyone gets a copy of August's new book,"

The crowd cheered loudly as if they won a million dollars. I remember the interview with the beautiful black man with the kaleidoscope eyes. His soft yet rough voice sent chills down my spine. He looked at me as if he was looking for an answer. He talked to me as if we were good friends, he knew too much, yet there was an ease being around him. While on tour *The Beautiful Ones* went into production, the story with Donatello and Josephine- I called Beef was also on its way.

Things seemed to be happening quickly. It seems like yesterday I stared at Adam complaining about my writers' block, and now I can't stop writing. I don't ever want to stop writing. There is serenity here, in my mind. Maybe because with the characters I am involved in their problems and not my own, I am escaping from reality. My reality. But my reality is not something that I need to escape from. I am living a good life. The life that I always wanted, being a successful author and watching my child grow up. I have no worries, bills are paid- on time. Joy is happy, what do I have to worry about in reality, but there is something special about the escape. I may not be Queen of the World, but when I write, I know the queen. Tommy introduces me to her and then tells me to write her story.

Joy came into my room. She was dressed and ready for camp. She wore a pair of dark demine shorts and a T-shirt that says, 2 Cute 2 Be 4 Gotten.

"Mom, let's go," she said to me.

She had her backpack full of items, her swimming suit, her towel, and flip-flops. With the July heat, she didn't want to spend a moment outside of the pool.

I sat up in bed.

"Where did you get that shirt?"

"Uncle X bought it for me," she told me proudly.

Since we been back home Joy has been sporting new clothes that my brother had given her. I told him.

"X, Joy doesn't need any more clothes. I don't have room to put them up,"

He ignores me and buys her whatever she points to.

I know I needed new clothes. I walked to my closet and saw the sight that makes everyone question me, my black wardrobe. I can't remember when I started to wear all black. I just knew that I invited to this function and that party and wearing black always seemed safe.

Considering that my book was in its second printing. Adam wanted to throw a party for me. He invited all of the big wigs, from investors, bankers, reporters, famous celebrities that actually read. The party was tonight.

Once I dropped Joy off at camp, I met DeAna for a shopping date. I kissed my sweet Joy goodbye, told her to have nice day, and then I went to X's bookstore for a free latte.

I found him behind the counter reading the newspaper. He peeked over the paper and grinned. I took a seat. One of his employees handed me my hazelnut latte.

"Your book is in demand," he said. "the one that is in production."

I nodded my head as I gently blew over the coffee. "What the problem, August."

"It's not my Gatsby," I said.

"Stop comparing yourself to other writers. Besides, Fitzgerald was a drunk in a bad marriage."

"I'm a single mother-,"

"Don't' compare I said." My brother cut me off. "Do Fitzgerald have his own latte,"

"No, but he has his own section in the libraries, and he is required reading in school."

"Look at the wall, there are posters of your book all over the place."

"You're August Schofield's little brother, of course, you have her posters up in your store."

Xavier shakes his head.

"I may be a little biased, but your work is good,"

"My work is good, but not great."

"Your work is great. Just mention the title of one of your books and the readers know."

"I don't want just the readers to know. Everyone knows who Fitzgerald is."

"So, you want to be a star?"

"No, just a great author."

Xavier placed a copy of Kirby Howard Magazine in front of me.

"Your interview was real good." He said. "A little evasive but good." I sipped my coffee. "Miles Palmer had nice things to say about you. I will let him distribute his magazine here. Did you read this?"

"No,"

"You should,"

I shrugged my shoulders.

"I gotta run X, I'm meeting Monique. You coming to the party tonight, right?"

"Yep," he answers. "I'll pick Sweet up and meet you at your place."

I left the bookstore to go meet Monique. We decided to meet at a local coffee shop near her home.

"Hi baby," she said smiling at me.

I smiled back.

We greeted each other with a hug.

"So, talk to me about the tour," she said as we sat down.

I shrugged my shoulders. "It was nice. I met Darnell Simpson. I went there overdressed. Folks were wearing shorts and flip-flops. We were eating ribs and drinking Faygo sodas." I laughed. Mo laughed too.

"Ms. Darnell was not drinking Faygo soda. You know she had wine and shrimp, big shrimp, colossal."

We laughed for a while, poking playful fun at the wealth of Darnell Simpson.

"Did you do any shopping or sigh-seeing?"

"Shopping for Joy, sightseeing-," I stopped talking to sip my coffee and quickly thought about the sights that I did see. Tommy Gibbs in the bathtub, Mr. William's Jazz lounge, *The Beautiful Ones* themselves were a sight.

"August, you didn't see anything," Monique fussed.

"I saw some stuff," I said.

"You saw nothing, and I am going to tell you why I know this because you have another book ready for release real soon."

"How do you know that book?" I asked, feeling busted in a lie.

"It's in the paper," she said to me.

I sighed.

"August, you're going to write your life away," she said shaking her head.

"I'll stop when I have my Gatsby,"

"You and that Gatsby, I swear August, you're going to kill yourself. If F. Scott Fitzgerald was alive, he would tell you to get over yourself.","

"Mo, that is not the same thing, I don't want to write *The Great Gatsby,* but I want my own great novel, I want to be among the greats, like Fitz."

"Okay then die, besides the greats are not legends until they're dead."

"Salinger was living with the success of The *Catcher in the Rye,*"

"So, you're obsessed with JD. Salinger now?"

"No,"

"You stress out about the wrong things. When was the last time you got laid?"

"I don't remember," I confessed.

"You know when the last time I got laid?"

"Knowing you, last night,"

"This morning," she said to me smiling. "That is your problem. Instead of basking in your success enjoy the fact that you don't have to go to a nine to five job, you are stressing about silly and insignificant matters. Stop looking at what you don't have but enjoy what you do have. Not everyone has the prettiest little girl in the world. Joy is beautiful. I read the article that Miles Palmer wrote." She said.

I shrugged my shoulders.

"That interview seemed weird," I said.

"Why?"

"I don't know, come let's go shopping for this party," I said.

**IN THE BOUTIQUE, I** live vicariously through Dominque she was my naughty big sister. Instead of scolding me whenever I did wrong, she would encourage me to be mischievous and naughty.

"What kind of outfit are you looking for?" she asked.

"Something nice but not too fancy, I'm not going to a ball, but something suitable," I said.

As we shop, I think about Gatsby, the concept of Gatsby and how do I write my own. With *The Great Gatsby*

The book started out with mixed reviews. It was after his death, and it was the next generations of readers that crowned the book to be a masterpiece. He wasn't trying to write a masterpiece; he was trying to earn a paycheck. It makes me think; when you're desperate, it seems as if you write better. You want to elaborate more, and the characters are so real it is as if you knew them. F. Scott coined a term, the Jazz Age, how significant is that. To put a collection of work in a category that you created. Most writers write about what they know or what they want. F. Scott wanted to live the American Dream, he wanted to be the underdog that made it. His wife didn't consider him until he had some money, like Daisy in *The Great Gatsby*. Was that why this book was so special because it was something that he dealt with?

My work doesn't reflect some kind of struggle for success. My characters are somewhat successful. They are not worried about paying the rent. They are not wondering where their next meal is coming from. They have money. Is that why I don't' have a Gatsby, because there is no quest for some kind of ideal dream. Is that why I have not reached Gatsby success?

Gatsby was a what if story. The kind of stories that I write, but there aren't any great loves, I don't need to gain riches to prove anything to anyone. I just want to write, to live out my dream as a successful writer. I die at the age of one hundred and ten, with my great grandchildren around me. I would be proud of my accomplishments and be proud of theirs. I would have a great American novel under my belt. I look up to a legend. Fitzgerald to me seemed smooth and charismatic. What am I missing?

I can't understand why I am not where I think I should be. Because not only do I look up to a legend, but I am named after a legend. August Wilson was a remarkable play writer. My parents made sure that Xavier and I had everything. We didn't want for anything. My mom died when X and I were young, but for the short time we had her, we never wanted.

The days when I was hungry and remembering if the sun would shine. It was while I was married to Joy's father. The mental and emotional abuse that he put me under all for the sake of showing off his power was beyond traumatic. One didn't know what mood he was in when I came home from work. I had to work to make sure we ate; he didn't want to work. If I wanted new clothes or wanting to buy something new, my motives were questioned. If I made an attempt to make myself look pretty; who was I looking nice for? Friends were forbidden. They represented laughter and blissfulness, and there was a strange fact that they may make see the abuse I was under.

My ex-husband was from the streets and whenever he was mad at me for any reason, he let me know that he was not a punk. My opinion meant nothing. If I didn't agree with what he had to say, then I was a sorry excuse for a wife.

Why did I say in such a mess? Considering where we lived, money seemed to hinder any chances of happiness, so as soon as we would get a little bit of extra money, things would be okay, but not for long.

One day I started to write again. I don't remember why I stopped, but I revisited the place that my brother calls the Land of Aug. There was serenity in the Land of Aug.

Then I noticed that there was no light in Joy's eyes, it was if she was dying. The atmosphere had to change, so I packed my bags and my baby and left. I moved in with X and focused on getting my life back together. I published my first book and moved to New York. I never looked back.

**"AUGUST-," DOMINIQUE CALLS MY** name.

I look at her.

"Where are you?"

I shake my head and look at my surroundings. I am in a restaurant.

"What the-," I questioned. "When did we get here?"

"You zoning out," she snaps

"What time is it?"

"It's one in the afternoon," she said. "You are not good company,"

"I'm sorry, but I don't remember not being here,"

She shakes her head and then looked over her menu.

"What seems to be your problem and don't give that Gatsby stuff either. I know what your problem is, you need a man in your life."

"I don't need a man," I tell her.

"With a man in your life, you wouldn't have this obsession about Gatsby,"

The waiter comes to the table to bring our drinks- that I didn't remember ordering. Dominique ordered her a martini and me a glass of ice water.

"Are you guys ready to order?"

"Yes," Dom said. "I would like the T-Bone steak with the loaded baked potato and broccoli,"

"I want a buffalo chicken salad with ranch, oh and black olives," I told him.

The waiter nods his head, collects our menus, and then leaves.

"What is your issue with men?" Dominque asks.

"No issue, I just don't have time to date." I defend.

My friend looks at me. Her eyes are intense as if she is trying to read something.

"Joy's father," she comments.

I briefly glance out the window,

"No," I said looking back at her.

"I know that when trust is broken-,"

"Dom," I interrupted. "Joy's father was an SOB, yes but I am okay, okay,"

"Okay," she said sipping her drink.

"You've been in New York for a while now, it seems like we have been friends forever," she reached out and touched my hand. "I just noticed that whenever a man takes notice of you, you back away and shut down."

"It's nothing," I said. "I admit, I am enjoying being single. Besides, I am too busy right now."

"Too busy in this great quest for Gatsby? I tell you what August, I will be so glad when you find him."

"Dominque, when did you realize that you were a great stylist?"

"When I was featured in *Vogue* magazine."

"See that is what I am talking about," I said.

"August, read the paper. Your books are number one; best sellers."

"Commercial success. No one is moved by my work. If I am so good how come Oprah hasn't called?"

"You want Oprah to call?" Dominique asks with a chuckle.

"I don't care who calls." I chuckle.

"You need a man to call." She scoffs.

"It's been so long, I would know what to do if a man does call."

I thought about Tommy in the bathtub with me, I chuckled to myself.

"Seriously D, I am someone's mother. You know what my plans are after we're done and besides the book party. My plans are to hear all about Joy's day at camp. Which kid peed in the pool, who hogged the black crayon, who was crowned champion of bean bag race-,"

"Okay, okay, August, I get it. Dating is somewhat of a challenge for single mothers."

"I promise, as soon as a get a nice piece of tail, you'll be the first to know."

DOMINIQUE FUSSES AS SHE goes through my closet. She fusses about my lack of color, and she fusses about why I have very few dresses. I have a lot of jumpsuits, but not a lot of dresses. I ignore her. I get dress in a sleeveless, black satin belted wide leg jumpsuit. I wear a silver chain necklace with a red Swarovski heart charm and matching bracelet. My hair pulled back into a ponytail; my bangs are feathered. I wear silver Swarovski studded earrings. My heels, black patented leather five-inch platform heels by Louboutin . My makeup, I do my own. I was a make-up artist in my former life. I studied Kim Kardashian's make up tutorial for a smoky eye. I will admit, I am quite impressed with how I put my outfit together.

I look into the mirror to give myself a final look, I see Tommy's reflection from the mirror. He sits on my bed, he starts to laugh,

*Now what?* I ask.

He shrugs his shoulders as if there is nothing he can do about his appearance. I turn to Dominique fussing about my wardrobe. I look back at Tommy. To my surprise he is holding a baby in his arms, a baby girl. She wears a pink bow in her jet-black curly hair. The scent in my room goes from perfume to baby powder. The baby was adorable. She sleeps peacefully as she sucks on a pacifier. Then a man, a young man walks into my room. He has dark tussled hair, and he is tall, standing at least six feet.

But what I notice the most are his eyes. He looks tired and sad. Next, entering my room is an older, petite full-figured woman.

"Justin," she said to the man.

He turns to face her,

"Get some rest. I'll take care of the baby,"

She reaches out to Tommy to hand her the sleeping baby. Once the baby is in her arms, she cuddles and kisses her forehead and then Justin, and she left my room.

I hold my breath. I don't want to go anywhere. I need to stay with Tommy and write and figure out who these people are. Who is that pretty baby? The smell of baby powder is intoxicating. I love the way a baby smells. I remember those days with Joy. She now smells like candy and milk. Justin, why is he sad? Or why did he look sad? Why did he need rest? Where was the baby's mother?

Then suddenly, almost like a blink of the eye, the scenery changed. I am no longer in my room but in a church.

People are crying softly. I look in front of the church and see a casket. As I walk slowly to the casket, I see a beautiful woman lying inside. She looks peaceful as if she is sleeping. I turn to look at the mourners; her family is crying. I see Justin holding the baby, tears fall from his eyes. I then realized that lying in the casket is the baby's mother. I close my eyes, feeling the pain of these mourners. How sad to lose someone so young? I wanted to cry, that poor pretty little baby. She doesn't have a mommy. I opened my eyes and looked to the pretty little baby. I am surprised to see how alert she is. She looks as if she understands everything. I walked to the baby and kneeled down before her. She reaches her hand out to me. I realized that this was her story.

I have to figure out what is going on. I have to get to know this baby. From the way her eyes look as if she knows what is going on. She is only a week old. What does a baby know after a week?

**"AUGUST,"**

I look up and see Dominique standing over me. I am sitting down on my bed. I looked around for Tommy. He is sitting next to me.

"Your car is here," she says to me.

I nodded my head.

X. is standing in the doorway.

"You, okay?"

I nodded my head.

**WE, DOMINIQUE, JOY, X**, and I and Tommy arrived at my party, Joy, Tommy. Joy cheers when she sees the elegant decorations. The ballroom is decorated black and white. There are round tables with white table clothes, black silk napkins, black square plates and red candles in the center that surrounds with red floral arrangements. The place is crowded full of reporters, photographers, journalists, bookstore owners, investors, other writers, fans, and to my surprise celebrities. I am speechless.

"Mommy, this looks like a ball!" she said as she smiled.

"There she is!" Adam replies, waving his hand to me.

I wave back

"August come over here!"

"Go," My brother said, "I have Sweet,"

I nodded my head, kissed Joy on the cheek, and walked to Adam. He greets me with a hug.

"Gold, baby, gold," He said to me.

"August," I hear someone call out.

I turned to the voice. It is a photographer wanting a picture. Together Adam and I pose for a picture, and then he escorts me through the room shaking hands and meeting people.

"August, *The Beautiful Ones,* is already in high demand." He begins.

I take a deep breath then slowly exhale.

"Really," I ask.

"Yes," he said. "As a matter of fact, TRS Studios wants to make a movie of *The Beautiful Ones-*,"

"But the book is not out yet, what if no one likes it."

"That is the thing, baby, it is predicted to be a best seller," Adam said to me, smiling. "Like music, a single is already dropping at number one."

I hesitate to continue.

"We will talk about it later," he said. "Tonight is about the second printing of this current book. So come let me introduce you to a few people."

ON ADAM'S ARM, HE introduces me to several of his personal friends and colleagues. I shake hands with the journalists, celebrities and all the people of note and thank them for coming out. I am compliment to the highest form with my latest work, and they ask me when the next book is coming out.

"Soon," Adam answers for me.

"What was your inspiration, August?" Journalist asks me.

I grin and answer

"I find my inspirations in the most unlikely of places."

"Looking forward to the next book, congratulations on your success," is what would be said afterward.

Every person that Adam had me to meet, I thank them, but I am very nervous because Tommy is standing behind me. This is the longest that he has been with me in the world of reality.

As I circulate throughout the party, I look for Joy. Is she okay? I have been meeting and greeting several people throughout the night. I begin to feel like I am neglecting her. As I look at her standing with Xavier, she appears to be okay. I grin at him as he meets and interacts with the guest.

I started to get antsy. My desire to write was stronger, stronger than ever. As thankful and grateful as I am to be here at this event, I did not want to be here. I close my eyes and take a deep breath. I open them, and the scenery has changed. I am in the living room. I see Justin lying on the couch, he is wearing black slacks and a black shirt. Jerica, the pretty baby, is sleeping on his chest. The petite woman, Marlene, who is Justin's mother, comes in from the kitchen wearing an apron.

"Justin, would you like me to fix you something to eat," she says to him.

She sits down on the love seat looking at him.

"You have to eat, honey." She encourages him.

He sighs. Coming from the upstairs is another man. He resembled Justin, it is his brother Joshua. In his arms, he holds a baby girl. She looks to be at least one. The little girl is beautiful. She is half Chinese, and her eyes are light brown. Her parents call her Amber. Amber's mother comes from the kitchen.

"Mama!" the baby calls out.

"Joshua, I'll take her." The baby's mother said.

Joshua hands Amber to her mother. He smiles at her, his wife.

"Thanks, Evelyn."

"I am going to pick up more diapers for Amber," Joshua says to his wife. Anything else that we need?"

Justin's eyes scan the room; he looks at his mother and brother.

"I'm trying to get him to eat," Marlene says.

Within moments, three men come in from the outside. Dominick, his wife, and their baby. Dominick has sandy blond hair and hazel-colored eyes. Dominick's wife's name is Rita. Their baby is D.J., Dominick Jr. He is two years old. Coming from a back room which may have been a den is Dylan, his wife whose name is Jury is not with him, she is in the den with their daughter also named Dylan. Dylan has dark hair and dark eyes. He has a square jaw, and his body is built from lifting weights. Next, coming in from the kitchen area is Jamie, another gentleman. Like Dominick, he had sandy blond hair, but his eyes are blue, beautiful sparkling blue eyes. Jamie is holding a baby. The baby appears to be at least one years old. I notice as everyone enters the living room with their babies Jerica wakes up from her nap. Justin notices that she is awake. He sits up, gently holding her in his arms.

"Want me to take her?" Marlene asks.

Justin shakes his head.

"I want to be alone." He says.

"Justin-," his friend replies, trying to reject his comment.

"No, seriously," Justin said. "For two weeks you've been hovering. I can't think with all you here."

The boys looked at each other, their wives glanced at each other.

"We're not leaving you alone," Dylan said. "Not this early,"

Justin begins to feed Jerica a bottle. Marlene sits down beside him.

"We cannot just be here," Dominick said to Justin as he sat down in the recliner. "Eva was special to us too."

"We need to be here, with you," Joshua said to his brother.

Justin doesn't reply. He looks at Jerica as nurses on the bottle.


I shake my head trying to focus again on the party.

*August don't fight it,* Tommy says.

*Why are you still here?* I ask.

*August, I told you, I am in here.* He says pointing to his head.

*I know that, but I am at a party. I have reporters and people all here to see me. I can't be goofy, not tonight.*

Tommy stands in front of me.

*Creative multitasking is how legends are born. He says with intensity in his eyes.*

His words ignite me, running chills through my body. It is if I have been bestowed special powers - creative writing powers.

*Will this be my Gatsby?* I ask myself.

Tommy chuckles as if my quest for Literary Domination is unfathomable.

**"HELLO," A VOICE STARTLES** me.

I turned around and see Miles Palmer standing before me. I grin.

"How are you?" he asks.

"Good," I answer.

Miles takes in a deep breath he looks around.

"This is a good turn out," he replies.

"Yeah," I said. "I'm surprised,"

"Why?" he asks putting his hands into his pockets.

I shrugged my shoulders.

"You don't think you're worth all this?" Miles ask.

"I'm not saying that" I answer.

"August, no one writes like you do. Your style is not standard. You have set a bar."

"How so?" I ask.

"You produced masterpieces like that," he snaps his fingers. "While others take years to produce quality literature in days."

My heart jumps which cause me to cough.

"What makes them classic?" I ask.

"Because they're timeless, already timeless."

I am beginning to get short-winded, Miles notices.

"Are you all right," he asks.

"Yeah, it's stuffy in here," I tell him.

"Come on, let's get some air."

I let Miles escort me outside, but with the New York summer air did offer much comfort.

"Can I get you some water?" he asks.

"No, no," I answer. "I'm okay,"

I am slowly beginning to regain my composer. I look at him.

"I'm sorry," I apologize.

"For what?" he asks with a chuckle.

*For being an idiot,* I want to say, but I just take in a deep breath.

"May I ask you something," he said.

"Shoot,"

"Are you a shy person?" he asks me to smile.

"No," I answer. "Why?"

Miles inhale and then exhales.

"I guess," he begins. "You seem very evasive and considering your success, and you're distant, you are either shy or-,"

My brother comes outside carrying my sleeping daughter in his arms.

"Partied hard," he says with a chuckle.

My brother looks at Miles.

"Xavier, you remember, Miles Palmer, editor, and chief-,"

"Oh yeah," X., said smiling. "Nice write up on my big sister."

Miles grins.

"Miles, my brother, Xavier Schofield," I said. "You have to excuse my kid brother. He is very biased when it comes to me,"

"As he should be," Miles says smiling. "I be proud too if my sister was a literary giant."

Miles looks at me with a grin.

I take a deep breath.

"Another interview," X asks.

"No, just needed some air," I answer. "Give me a minute, I'll tell Adam that we're leaving."

"No, no, I'll take Sweet home, enjoy the rest of your evening. I already have a cab coming."

"Um, okay," I say.

I watch as a cab pull up. I tell my brother goodnight and kissed my Joy on the forehead and then watch as they get into the cab and leaves.

"Your brother seems very proud," Miles comments.

"Proud is not the word," I said laughing. "He owns a bookstore and keeps my books right in front."

"My first issue of Kirby Howard, my mom had every page laminated and tried to put in the church bulletin."

I laugh.

"I noticed baby girl tonight. Joy seems lovely."

"She is," I said smiling.

Laughter roars from inside. I turn my head to the sound then look back at Miles. I need to get back to the party, but I don't want to leave him.

"Sounds like they're having a good time," he said.

"Yeah, right now, I rather be at home writing."

Miles chuckles.

"When are you not writing?"

"I can't honestly say when I am not writing. I can be sound asleep, have a dream, and I wake up and start writing."

"How does your writing interact with your muse?"

He is asking about Tommy again. Quickly I glanced around to see if Tommy was with me, but he wasn't. I look at Miles.

"Off the record," he asked with a grin.

"I'm going back inside," I said evasively.

I attempted to go back inside, but Miles stands in front of me.

"Why are you being so coy?" he asks.

"I'm not," I said. "But I told you before, I cannot answer that question."

His blue eyes are trying to read me. I could tell that my evasiveness is somewhat annoying. I feel bad that I am being so elusive about the situation, but I cannot talk about Tommy with no one.

"Read my work," I said. "that is the only answer that I can give you."

"August, why the wall?"

"Excuse me?" I ask.

Now I am somewhat annoyed.

"You have this wall up, why?" Miles asks.

My emotions go from annoyed to both surprised and amused. I am somewhat intrigued by his intrigue.

"I am not telling you to tell the world all your business, but-,"

"What do you want?"

His blue eyes stare at me with intensity.

"I want to know you, I like you," Miles said.

I am caught off guard. For the longest sixty seconds of my life, we looked at each other. Before I can respond, Adam comes outside.

"August, there you are," he says. "I've been looking all over for you. Hey Miles, how you doing?"

Adam extends his hand to Miles to shake.

"Good," Miles says to Adam, shaking his hand. "Awesome turn out."

"August, the execs from TRS are here," Adam informs me.

Adam doesn't wait for me to respond. He grabs my hand and pulls me back inside.

"Adam, I told you that I don't want to commit to anything when I am not certain."

"August, stop it. We will get the best writers to do the screenplay, the best director, producers, and cast. We are talking Oscar, and it is based from your book."

Still not waiting for a response, he pulls me to the executives of TRS Studio, Tye Smith and his daughter Tia. I shake their hands and thank them for coming.

"I am a big fan, Ms. Schofield," Tia said smiling.

"August," I told her.

"TRS studios would love to do a movie of your next work, *The Beautiful One*,"

"That's what I am told," I said, "but the book hasn't been released yet, I don't want to take a gamble on something that is not good."

"August, you are lucky number seven," Tye said to me.

"I don't gamble Mr. Smith," I said.

"Tye," he said to me. "And August, Adam said that the book is good, and based on the sales from your previous work, I don't think that a gamble will be too costly."

Tye, Tia, and Adam begin talking. I tune them out and see Justin and Jerica again. He is holding her in his arms. She looks as if she is six months. I looked around for Tommy. I see him standing in the distance. He nods his head to me to acknowledge this brainstorm. As I continue to appear that I am in conversation with Adam and the Smiths, I see a young lady walking towards Justin and Jerica. She carries a journal in her hands, and she looks upon them endearingly. It is at that moment that I realize that the young lady is Jerica, as an adult. How is this story going to flow?

To think, every time they celebrate her birthday, they are celebrating the anniversary of Eva's death. How does Justin deal with that? How does he cope with the fact that every time he looks into his baby's eyes, he is reminded that her mother is dead?

**"WELL," ADAM RESPONDS.**

I looked at him, not knowing how to respond because I had tuned everyone out.

"I'm sorry, ask me again," I said. "The noise,"

"We can discuss the details over lunch tomorrow," Tye suggests.

I thought I made my point clear about the movie.

"I have to check my schedule. Can I call you?"

"Sure," Tia says looking at her father. "Adam has our number,"

I shake hands with the execs, bid them good night and thank them again for coming, and Adam and I watch them leave. I quickly turned to Adam.

"Why are you pimping me?" I ask, blowing up at him.

"August, I am not pimping you," he replied with a chuckle. "They came by the office today wanting to know how they get in touch with you."

I sigh

"What, August,"

"I told you the first time you bought this movie deal up that I wasn't interested and now-,"

"Okay, okay, August, I just wanted you to meet with them. Listen, I noticed that you haven't eaten yet, want me to fix you a plate?"

I don't answer. Adam leads me to an empty table; I watch him leave to prepare a plate for me. I sat down. I looked at my watch and saw that it was after midnight. I am tired, but I am not ready to leave yet. I haven't had fun yet. I haven't danced or laughed with my friends. Throughout the evening, I saw Dominique interact with guests and do some networking, but with my hallucinations and Adam pimping me out to everyone, I didn't have much time to enjoy my party. I look across the room and to my surprise, Miles is still here. He walks to me and sits down.

"You're still here?" I said.

"Yep," he said looking at me. "I wanted to finish our conversation."

"Oh?" I ask confused.

Adam returned with a plate full of wing digs, and grilled shrimp on a skewer, and potato salad. He sets the plate in front of me and leaves. I offer Miles food, but he declines.

"What conversation are you talking about," I ask, as I began to devour my food.

I look at him then remember his intense intrigue of my muse. Before I can tell him again no comment, my attention focuses on the music that is playing. I close my eyes and begin to feel the rhythm of the music. I suddenly feel at ease, as if tension is released from my body. I look across the room and see Jerica dancing with her friends, D.J., and Baby Girl Dylan, she is called. She looks to be at least twenty-one. She is so free. As she dances as if there isn't a care in the world.

**"SO HOW ABOUT IT?" Miles asks.**

"What?" I asked.

"Tomorrow morning, how about some coffee,"

That is the conversation that he wanted to finish? Miles said that he likes me. I've been out of the dating game for a long time. I don't remember anything. I don't remember what the first kiss feels like or what it is like being held in someone's arms. I don't remember the feeling of the butterflies that swam in my stomach. Being in love, looking into a man's eyes and know that they love you too. For a man to hold me in their arms in their sweet embrace. I haven't been held in such a long time. To be kissed, I haven't been kissed in ages. To feel their soft lips against mine, to feel their warm breath against my cheek, my neck, it's been a long, long time. It's been a long time since I have had any kind of stimulation, but at this moment. I can't think about that, I want to write. I wanted to understand the dynamic about Jerica.

I look at Miles and see Tommy standing behind him. I think about going out for a latte technically isn't a date. And if we go to my brother's bookstore, we can have free lattes. The amount of time it takes to drink a latte is an hour. I can be back in my world of make-believe in no time.

"Why do I get the feeling that you're not here for a story?"

"A story?"

"You came out tonight to cover this event, right?"

"No," he said looking at me intently. "I came to see you,"

"Right, to inquire about this evening, why else would you ask about Tommy?"

"Because I want to get to know you,"

"For your story,"

"No," he said. "I want to get to know you for me,"

I look away now nervous. He likes me.

"If you're not interested-,"

"I didn't say that" I said quickly. "I think you're a real nice person,"

"But,"

172

"No buts-," I said,

Before I finish my brush off, Adam returns.

"August, I have someone I want you to meet," Adam said.

I grin and stand up.

"I ah, I'll talk with you later, okay."

Miles nodded his head into bow in defeat.

Adam takes me to whoever want me to meet. We chat briefly. I thank them for coming out and showing support, and I look at my watch,

"Adam, I need to get home, it's late."

"Okay, August,"

Adam leads me outside, and he raises his hand to summon the car; the same car that brought me tonight.

I enter my home and see my brother sleeping on the couch. I put a blanket over him and then I go to check on Joy. She is sleeping and snoring peacefully in her bed. I walk to her and kiss her on the cheek.

"Mom," she says waking up.

"Joy, go to sleep," I whisper.

Instead she sits up and I sits down on the edge of her bed.

"Why are you up?"

"I want a hug,"

I lean in and hug her.

"I love you, Joy,"

"I love you too, Mommy," she said back. "You going to get some sleep,"

I nodded my head.

"You look tired," Joy said to me.

"What does tiredness look like?" I ask.

She shrug her shoulders.

"Come on, lay down and go to sleep, camp tomorrow,"

I tuck her in, kiss her on the forehead again and the leave her room.

**AFTER MY SHOWER, I** dress in my pajamas. I walk into my room and as predicted, I see him standing by my window. I begin to wonder if the real Tommy read about my success or my books, is he a fan?

*We need to set some boundaries, I said to him. I can't have you in my head while I am working, networking. Here, while I am alone is fine, but-,*

*I am here when you are writing. You're the one that need to have some boundaries while you're writing.*

*I have boundaries, I defend.*

*If you had boundaries, then I wouldn't be here tonight, he says pointing to his head.*

I shake my head.

*He won't stop inquiring about you. I said. Why you're my muse.*

*He wants to know you. Tommy said.*

*No one else cares why you are my muse. Why him? I asks.*

*Because he likes you, he wants to get to know you. Tommy answers.*

*I can't entertain that right now. I said. I need to write. I just want to write my Gatsby. There are too many distractions.*

I sit down on my bed. Tommy sits next to me.

*My daughter told me that I look tired.*

*Then get into bed and get some sleep. No writing tonight.*

I climb into bed, and like a protective big brother, Tommy tucks me I and sits down beside me.

*Will you be here when I wake up?*

*Depends on you,*

Tommy lies down next to me. There isn't any physical attraction, just emotional comfort. There is peace in the Land of Aug. I knew my behavior is not normal. I'm not crazy, I just enjoy writing. Writing is my job; writing is my passion. Actors and actress want to win the Oscar, Emmy or Tony. Singers want to win the Grammy; I want to win the Gatsby.

I slept fitfully because my mind was on Jerica. Her daddy calls her Jeri or Baby Jeri. I saw her in my dreams, beginning as a five years old-year-old girl; Pretty little girl with thick, curly, jet-black hair; ringlets that hung in her eyes and she loved to wear overalls. D.J. and she are best friends. Naturally, Jeri was daddy's girl. He was putty in her hands. They would give each other Eskimo kisses.

*My father was quiet- I heard her voice. He wasn't one for many words.*

*What was he like? - I asked.*

*He was very generous, very sweet and lovely. He loved his family and his friends. Now Mama, my grandma, hated the fact that I was a tomboy, but she was amazing, she always hummed a song. She always had a song to sing. She had a soft spot for Amber, maybe because Amber was* girly-girl, she was a princess. Amber, she was my princess cousin.

I chuckled at Jerica's cynical tone in regards to her cousin.

But Mama loved me, she loved me very much.

When did you find out about your mom? I asked.

I always knew even as a baby.

How is that possible? -I questioned.

I don't know, I just knew that she gave up her life so that I could live. When I was born, I knew that she died. When my father first held me, we connected. The first time I actually saw my mom was in a photo that was mounted up on the wall I was six months old. I remember noticing the picture. I kept pointing to the photo, Daddy and Mama smiled.

"Does she recognize her?" Mama asked Daddy.

My father shrugged his shoulders

"Justin look at her," Mama said. "She recognizes Eva."

I looked at my father; I pointed to the picture again. My dad took me to the photo, I laughed. I was so excited because I was able to see her, to see what my mom looked like. I touched the picture. My father was shocked that I knew who my mom was.

"Say Mommy," he said softly in my ear.

"Ma-," I cried out.

I looked at Mama. She had tears in her eyes.

I leaned towards the picture and kissed her face. "Ma, Ma,"

"Justin, how does she know?"

"I don't know,"

*Immediately Mama grabbed a box of photos, Daddy sat me down and I watched as she sorted through them. She pulled a photo of my mom. It looked different from the one on the wall. I smiled at the phone, I said; "Ma,"*

*I looked at my father. I saw sadness in his eyes. I squirmed around so that I could face him. He turns me around to face him. I leaned in to kiss his nose; he smiled and then he kissed my nose.*

*Was this some kind of gift? I ask Jerica.*

*No, I don't think so. I just knew. I don't know how to explain it, but I just knew. My grandmother and father didn't have to tell me about her death.*

*What were birthdays like? I asked.*

*Very, very special. We have cake, and ice creams, balloons, family and friends and at the end of the night, Daddy would like a candle for Mom,*

*"Thank you for our baby," he would say.*

*"Thank you for my life," I say.*

*We would sit back and watch the flame flicker. My mom's spirit was always with me. I could feel her presence.*

This story was a unique story, about a girl's whose mother, although dead, was always around.

I WAKE UP EARLY IN the morning to write. I get dressed and wait for Joy. Once she is ready for camp, we are off.

"We're making masks today," she says smiling.

"You're going to make me a mask," I ask.

"Nope," she said quickly. "I am going to make it for my uncle."

"I want a mask too, Joy,"

"You don't need one, Mom." Joy said to me. "My camp counselors are reading your books. I said. 'My mom made that book,', then Devon said. 'Nu-uh, your mom didn't make nothing.', Mommy, I don't like him. I said, 'My mom made that book, and she is number one, and she has coffee in Pixburgh,', Devon got mad and stomped away."

"Joy, be nice," I warn.

"I am nice, but he was talking about you like you a nobody! Nobody is going to speak bad about my mommy."

Joy, The Great Defender.

"Joy, you don't have to defend me," I said with a chuckle.

She stops walking. She looks up at me.

"I love you, Mommy." She said.

"I love you too, Joy," I said smiling.

I drop Joy off and kiss her goodbye and then walk to X's for my latte. I find him perched at the counter, reading the newspaper and having his breakfast, which is scrambled eggs, bacon, toast and green tea.

"What time did you get in last night?" Xavier asks, handing me my latte.

"I don't remember," I answer.

"It was a nice event," he says.

I shrugged my shoulders.

"What-,"

"Last night proved that I do good work," I answer.

"But-,"

"Nothing," I said, then sighed. "What is good in the news?"

"Nothing," X said folding up the paper.

He then grins and sips his juice.

"Miles Palmer seems to be cool," Xavier comments.

"X, you only like him because he wrote a great review about me."

"That means he's smart." Xavier comments, smirking. "All joking aside, he looks at you as if he really likes you. You know I would like more nieces and nephews, maybe one name after me,"

"Xavier," I admonish.

"August, relax!" Xavier laughs. "I am not that much younger than you. I remember the days when boys were itkey and gross. Are they gross to you? Do you like women?"

"X!" I exclaim.

"August, I am trying to find out what is going on with you, you don't date, you daydream for hours, my niece eats dry cereal."

"She likes it!" I snap.

I caught myself. I take a deep breath and then sip my coffee. Xavier chuckles at my outburst.

"I am a writer, a bestselling author," I said, more poised and calmer.

Xavier looks at me, his eyes are trying to read me. He is reading my mind. I look away and sip my latte again.

"You're going to kill yourself." He said, coolly.

"I'm fine," I reply. "Xavier, I am a single, working, a mother."

"Okay," Xavier says coolly.

"I gotta go, X. See ya later," I said.

I grab my latte and leave.

I look at my cell phone and see that I have numerous messages from Adam. I want to scream. I know what they are about, the meeting with the TRS execs. One would think that my aloof demeanor is evident that I am not interested. I have three books written, three books in a matter of two months, and if I add Jerica's story that will be four. I have fulfilled my contract with Adam. I can renew my contract or find another publisher. I'll make sure that Adam is aware of that next time he forces my hand, especially with TRS.

I slowly stroll along the city in no particular rush to go anywhere, it's actually nice that I don't have to rush home to write because Jerica's story had been written permanently in my mind. As I continued to walk, I passed a small café. There is a middle-aged woman sitting down eating what appeared to be a muffin, and she is drinking coffee. What catches my eye is what was in her hands. She is reading a book- my book. I stand frozen, stunned by what I see. I don't know what to think. I mean, I know people are reading my work, but I just never saw them reading. She looks intense as if she is reading a good part. What part is she on? Suddenly, I am filled up with so much anxiety that it feels like I am going to bust. I have to move. If she sees me staring, she may think that I am some weirdo, but I can't move from my spot.

"August," I hear someone from behind me, startling me.

I turn around to see a familiar face- those eyes. The sun makes them look almost transparent. He is smiling at me.

"What's up? Thought you would have slept in after last night."

"No, not with an energetic kid," I said with a chuckle. "What are doing here?"

"My office is a block away."

"Look," I said with excitement, pointing to the woman in the café. "She's reading my book,"

"August, you're a bestselling author," Miles said with a chuckle.

"Yeah, but I never saw someone reading my book," I said looking at him. "Do you think she's enjoying it?"

"It looks like it,"

I want to know if she likes the book. Maybe Miles can ask her. I look at him. His eyes see what I am conjuring up. He takes a deep breath and quickly says:

"No,"

Miles attempts to walk away.

"Please," I said grabbing his arms.

I am suddenly caught off guard by his biceps- he has muscles. I quickly let go of his arm and refocus on my request.

"I have to know," I plead.

"August you already know," he said.

He pulls a newspaper from his bag,

"Look at the New York Times, you are still in the bestseller's list. I am sure that she likes your book,"

"Those are from statistics from sales, but here is someone actually reading my work, please Miles,"

Miles look offended.

"What?"

"I'm a fan, have you ever asked me if I liked your work?"

I look at him; the sun shifts behind the clouds making his eyes the color of aqua.

"Your opinion doesn't count, because you like me. Whatever you have to say is bias-,"

"Are you serious," he asks, even more offended. "What is the matter with you?"

I can't respond.

"Are you always this-," he hesitates.

"Off-centered, yep! Weird, yep! I am a bit neurotic, yep! I have to know that I am not writing to be writing, that I am making a contribution to literature. Numbers mean nothing to be. Anyone can get numbers, but it takes one great act to make someone a legend. If I know that someone likes my book, and really enjoys my gift of writing, then I know I am okay, I fulfilled my purpose."

He looks away as if to think about what I said. I wait. I look in the window and see the lady has finished her muffin and her coffee. She has packed up her book and left. Miles sees that she has left too. I am stuck. I can't move. Miles finally looks at me.

"Come with me," he said.

He begins to walk down the street. Slowly and reluctantly, I follow him. We don't talk as we walk down the street.

WE WALK INSIDE A building then take the elevators up two flights, once the doors open, I realize that I am in the headquarters of Kirby Howard. I see a few people going to and from, doing miscellaneous activities saying good morning to one another and Miles. I heard some people whisper my name. I follow Miles into his office. He set his bag down and motioned his head for me to come to him to his bookshelf. I slowly walked over. He points to the section where all of my books are and pulls out my first book. It looks worn and tattered.

"I can't tell you how many times I read this book." He says. "This was before I knew that you were female. This book is so good. I'm an avid reader, I love the classics, love the new stuff. My feelings for you has nothing to do with this book. Now when I first saw you at the restaurant with your friends. I knew that I want to know you, August the woman. Plus, I wanted to meet August the author. There is only one Michael Jordan, practice your jump shots, slam dunks, and free throws. August Schofield, the Queen of the Scene. August, no one has ever captured a scene like you do. You have made your contribution."

I watch as Miles put his book back.

"Now I want to get to know the woman. I can see it will be a challenge," he said with a laugh.

I sigh then walk to the large bay window. Miles follows me. I turned to him. He smiles.

"It's cool if you don't like me."

"No," I laughed. "I'm not good at dating,"

His eyes ask why.

"I rather write then socialize."

Again, his eyes asked why.

"I can't explain this, as a matter of fact, this is something I am trying to figure,"

Miles' telephone rang. He excuses himself to answer the phone. I slowly walk around the office looking at everything. There are pictures on his wall. One is a poster from the movie Scarface, I chuckle at that one. There are photos of him and famous celebrities.

"Do you have plans this afternoon?" Miles asks as he hangs up the phone.

"Why?"

"My interview was canceled," he said walking to me. "And I don't have any pending meetings, maybe we can hang out, spend the day together,"

I take a deep breath. Miles sensed my hesitation.

"This doesn't have to be a date," he replies. "Since you have some type of trepidation when it comes to dating."

"No, there is nothing trepidations about my dating phobia," I defend myself. "I ah, would love to date, to have the possibility of spending time with someone, but-,"

"But what?"

"My schedule is busy," I said.

"Is it really?" he asks with doubt. "I just saw you wondering the streets of New York, stalking women in the coffee house."

I playfully glared at him.

"That is different," I said. "I was going for a walk after I dropped Joy off at camp and I happened to see that woman. Anyway, I am a full-time writer and a full-time mom."

"When do you make time for you?"

"Whenever I write," I said then chuckled.

I look back at the window.

"My friends have been staging interventions."

"What-," Miles asks with a laugh.

"I don't socialize enough, is what they're saying. They also think because of my marriage, I stopped socializing, and I bury myself in my work."

"What happened?"

I take a deep breath and look at him.

"He wasn't very nice," I said, being diplomatic.

Miles slowly nod his head.

"But he's not the reason why it may seem that I am reluctant to date, it's just-," I try to find the words to elaborate.

How does one explain that I rather live in my mind? I look at him,

"Writing has just become my life. I try not to be stand-offish or reclusive, but whenever I get inspired about a new idea, I must be left alone to write."

Miles grins.

"Would you like me to show you around?"

"Sure,"


*Kirby Howard,* the magazine began with Miles' love for artist expression. He loves art, he loves musicals, he loves social news, he loves fashion, and of course, he loves literature. He introduces me to some of the members on his staff. One guy, in particular, Matthew Gibson, one of the literary editors of the magazine.

"Very nice to meet you," Matthew said shaking my hand.

"The pleasure is mine." I reply.

"Who are some of your influences?" Matthew asks.

"Fitzgerald, Morrison," I answer.

"You know it would be an honor if you did an editorial," Matthew suggests, smiling.

"I'll think about it," I reply, with a nervous chuckle.

Miles must have sensed my apprehensiveness.

"Well, Matt, thank Ms. Schofield for stopping by," Miles says.

"Thanks, Ms. Schofield," Matthew said sounding like a child.

I laugh, and Miles and I walk back to his office.

I feel my stomach growl. I checked my watch and see that it is after eleven a.m.

"I'm hungry," I comment. "Want to get something to eat, my treat,"

Miles chuckles,

"If I am the one who wants to date you, shouldn't I be the one paying?"

I take a deep breath.

"Okay," I said slowly. "Pizza?"

"Okay," Miles said with a grin. "I know this great pizzeria."

"Okay," I take a deep breath.

"No pressure, we'll just hang out, cool?"

Pizza with no commitments, I think I can handle this.

**I SIT ACROSS FROM** Miles, and I try not to phase in and out. I try to stay focused and listen to him talk. Miles has a sister named Lena married, with two children, twin boys named Mason and Jason. At 37 years old, Miles had never been married, and he didn't have children. Talking with him seems easy and looking at him, is like watching at an Arizona sunrise. The sunlight makes his eyes change to different shades of blue, from blue topaz to aquamarine, and then my favorite color light color. His skin is the color of caramel when the sun shines upon him his skin looks copper. His voice is deep, but soft-his voice draws me in. He has the type of voice that is soothing, the kind that I want to talk sweetly to me in the middle of the night, while we lay under the covers.

I feel fluttering in my stomach. Chills run through my body as I look at him. Do I like him? I haven't liked a man in a long time.

**WE LEAVE THE PIZZERIA** and with no particular place to go. We stroll through Central Park.

My cell phone rang, it was Adam, but I don't answer it. I grunt.

"Is everything all right?"

"Yeah," I sigh.

"What's the matter?" Miles asks.

"Adam wants me to turn my next book into a movie," I tell Miles.

He looks impressed.

"It would increase book sales; not that you would need it-,"

"What if the book isn't good," I say quickly. "They want a book that hasn't been released yet,"

"Your work has a good reputation. I am sure that it will work out all right," Miles said with a chuckle. "August, image your characters coming to life."

*Them coming to life is not the problem,* I say to myself.

"I think this will be a good step for you," Miles encourages. "Plus, you can have full creative control."

My cell phone rings again.

"Is that him?" Miles ask with a chuckle.

I nod my head,

"Yep, excuse me," I sigh, "Yes, Adam,"

"Why have you not returned my calls," he snaps.

""I've been busy, what do you want?"

"TRS tonight at the Four Seasons," he states.

"I'm not, I-,"

"Shut up," he yelled. "I will kill you,"

"Stop threatening me!" I yell. "I'll be there."

I hung up the phone.

"Was he threatening to kill you?" Miles asks.

"It's his way of showing his love," I answer with sarcasm.

"He seems interesting,"

"He keeps me young," I reply. "He has me going to the Four Seasons tonight to discuss this so-called movie deal. I need to get home, so I can mentally prepare myself for this,"

"Okay," he says with a grin.

"Today was nice," I said with a grin.

I took a deep breath and then exhaled.

"Yeah, it was okay," I said.

Miles grins,

"I'm glad," he replies. "Can I see you again, maybe when it is a little darker out, a little candlelight."

I chuckle and then nod my head. He smiles at me.

"Cool," he says.

I don't know if I should try to hug him, shake his hand, or try to kiss him. Shaking his hand seems too impersonal, hugging him may send mixed signals, and as far as kissing him; if he kisses the way he looks, I could pass out right in the middle of the park. Before I could solve my own issue with how to end this afternoon, Miles leans and kisses me on the cheek. His soft lips send an electrical current through me. Quickly, I inhale

"I'll call you tomorrow," he says to me.

I nod my head, still feeling tingly sensation from his gentlemen like embrace. Miles flags down a cab; I get inside and go home.


**TYE AND TIA SMITH** and Adam at the Four Seasons watch me enter the Four Seasons. They smile brightly, like that cat in Alice in Wonderland. They stand as I approach the table as if I am a queen or something.

"Thank you for meeting with us," Tye said shaking my hand.

They make room for me to sit, and together the four of us sat down; them surrounding me.

"August we are looking forward to working with you," Tia said.

I grin as I look over the menu. A waiter comes to our table with vintage wine. I put my hand over my glass, indicating that I don't want any wine.

"Just ice water, please."

"Not a drinker?" Tye asks, smiling.

"No," I said with a grin.

**WE EAT APPETIZERS, SHRIMP** cocktail, stuffed mushrooms, and sizzling scallions, Tye and Tia tell Adam and me about their start in the movie industry. I dip my shrimp in the cocktail sauce. TRS Exec and Adam look at me, I think they are waiting for me to jump at their idea. My eyes shift to the waiter approaching our entrees. I watch with the waiter sets everyone's entrée in front of them. As we eat our food, I listen to Adam and the TRS Execs make idle chit-chat. I still have not made a decision on wanting to sell my rights to my book.

"I am not very uncomfortable with the idea that my book is not available yet." I said.

Tye chuckled. My statement seemed comedic and irrational. "Sorry,"

"August," Tye begins, "I know this is very overwhelming-,"

"It's beyond overwhelming," I state abruptly. "Listen, it has been nice meeting you both, but I am not deciding on anything especially not this early."

Tye and Tia look at each other and then look at me and smile.

"Okay," they both say to me.

"August, if you want to wait after the year of the release, two years. That is fine. We want to work with you. My father and I own our own studio, we work on our time. No one else's."

I smile at Tye. I want to thank her for understanding.

**AS WE DINED ON** dessert, I think about the movie adaptations of *The Beautiful Ones.* I must admit, I am curious to see who would play who. How many actors and actress will line up for the part? I can hear their agents calling Tye and Tia requesting an audition. I begin to think of the score. The type of music that would be playing in the background. My mind began to wonder about *The Beautiful Ones.* I want a good score, like from the movies, Rocky and the Karate Kid. The kind of score that gets you excited. I know that every time I hear the *Rocky* score, I am ready to run around Philadelphia like a champion boxer.

I remember being so mad at *The Beautiful Ones* because they are vain and emotionally destructive. I was almost embarrassed to be associated with them because I am not vain or emotionally destructive, but suddenly, I became fascinated with them again and suddenly I see Tommy sitting in between Tia and Tye. I chuckled at how out of placed he looked.

**ADAM AND I SIT** alone at the table, he sips on brandy and I had a cranberry juice.

"No longer obsessed with the quest for Gatsby?" Adam asks.

"I'm always obsessed with the Gatsby," I confess with a smile.

"When was the last time you slept?" Adam asks.

"You know Joy said that same thing!" I exclaimed shocked.

Adam chuckles.

"Joy, wow. You know you need sleep if your baby is recommended it."

I nod my head.

"When was the last time you have a vacation, no writing, no working, just relaxing."

"I was a teenager," I answer, then chuckled.

"August, this is your season to reap the harvest, to enjoy your success as August Schofield. I know you have noticed your contract,"

I nod my head.

"We can do another three-book deal, but I am afraid to because you have been spitting books out left and right. Your contract will be up in a month."

We both laugh.

"So, what do we do?" I ask.

"I'm not letting you go. God forbid that you go to another publisher-,"

"Don't worry, Adam. You own my soul." I say to him sadistically.

"Haha," Adam commented. "Seriously, I enjoy our relationship, but I am not going to renew your contract until I know that you're okay. I want you to go on vacation for a while relax,"

"Sounds ideal, but you cannot tell a writer not to write," I said. "We're always thinking about an idea."

"August, relax, you have more than enough books and royalties coming to enjoy some time for yourself. Listen to me, one month, while Joy is still out for the summer, sightsee, wear those ugly tourist clothes; you know color in your wardrobe. Send me a postcard. When you come back, we can talk about a new contract."

I sigh.

We shared a cap, once the cap pulled up to my brownstone. Adam walks me to my door. He kisses me on the cheek and bids me good night.

**I ENTER MY HOME and** see my brother sleeping on the couch again. I put a blanket over him and went to check on Joy. I get to her room to find her peacefully sleeping. Like the night before, I can feel Tommy's presence. I take a long hot shower and try to think of my next move. A vacation? Where in the world am I going to go? I just came back from California and Dallas, but I don't remember anything about it, because I was too busy writing. Rome, I can go to Rome, that is far away, and with the money I spend on the trip, I can't afford to not see. I can stay for two weeks. That is long enough for me to clear my head and not think of whatever pressure. However, the more I thought about not writing, more I wanted to write.

Writing calms, me, it makes things easier. When chaos and pandemonium stir around me like a tornado, I write. Whenever I write, there are rainbows. The bickering I hear from individuals around me sounds like a three-part harmony. Not all of my characters have bright and sunny days, and birds are not always singing, but for some reason, their lives seem more pleasant than the lives around me

**I ARRIVE AT MY** brother's bookstore for my latte and lecture.

"Your couch is murder on my back," he said.
"There is an extra room with a bed,"

"I know, I know, but fell asleep on the couch," he said. "What time did you get in?"

"Not until after midnight?" I answer. "But just in time for you to call them hogs," I joked with a southern dialect and began to making snoring noises.

My brother laughs.

"I take it that meeting went well,"

I nodded my head,

"Yep, they want to turn one of my books into a movie," I inform.

My brother smiles at me.

"I was advised to go on vacation. I am working too hard,"

"You, someone who has a permanent resident on the Land of Aug,"

"Ha ha," I commented. "I am thinking about going to Rome for a few weeks."

"You're not taking my niece to Rome," my brother said.

"First of all, my baby- eight and half hours of labor and no drugs, thank you very much. Second, come with me,"

"No, I have to maintain things here. I just came back from visiting our family in Pittsburgh. Why Rome?"

I shrugged my shoulders.

"Something exotic, fun,"

"Sounds nice, bring me back a T-shirt, I heart Rome or something. You're not taking Sweet,"

"Why not,"

"August, it is too far, she would need a passport, immunizations, too much for a little girl. You go, have fun, Sweet can stay with me."

"X; I'm the big sister!" I snap. "Listen, I can take my baby to the moon if I wanted, my baby,"

"I will put you on the moon," Xavier snapped back.

He takes in a deep breath.

"Seriously," Xavier begins. "You have been under some stress, lately, two successful books back-to-back, a book tour, second printing of a book that is only a few months old. You're going to need a stress free, kid free moment, and now the movie. Too much right now, and Sweet will be back in school soon."

"Exactly, I haven't spent that much time with her. Plus, I just can't go off somewhere living my Joy behind."

"August, Sweet ain't thinking about you,"

"Ouch!"

"August, she knows you have to write. I was hard on you before, but I see you are stressed out, and you're no good for her stressed."

"I just about had it with you calling me unfit," I warn.

"I am not saying you unfit." My brother defends himself. "Seriously, it's not like you're going for the year, just a few weeks, let her finish enjoying her summer, she made friends, some kid name Devon,"

"She told me she doesn't like him."

"Kids, best friends at twelve noon, enemies by one-thirty. Seriously, leave her here, she is fine."

I sip my latte and look through the part of the paper that my brother isn't looking through. Considering that I am somewhat forced into leaving my baby behind, I want to find something for her to do. I can take her to the zoo or the Met. As my brother talks about something, but I zone out. I see Tommy sitting down on a chair. I take a deep breath. He looks at me with a smile.

*I am supposed to be on a writing break.*

"August," I hear my name.

My brother calls me. I turned around to face him. I see a woman standing at the counter.

"Hi," I chuckle.

"Can you sign my book?" She asks.

"Sure,"

I signed the woman's book. Then she leaves the store. I look at my brother; he shakes his head at me.

"Bye X.,"

**I ENTER DOMINIQUE'S BOUTIQUE,** KingDoms. I find Dom and Linda, her assistant, organizing the jewelry counter. I love Dominique's boutique. The white walls and gold and glass chandelier. She has clothing racks full of clothes that she has brought for her clients. She travels everywhere for her clothes and accessories. I slowly walk to her jewelry table; Dominique shoots me a look;

"Back away from the table!" she jokes.

Linda laughs.

"I need clothes and jewelry for Rome." I tell her, my hands up surrendering.

"Rome," she asked. I nodded my head. "What's in Rome?"

"My sabbatical," I joke.

She laughs.

"Want to come?" I ask.

"Rome?" she asked, with a grin. "Really?"

I nodded.

"Seriously, why are you going to Rome?" Dominique asks, approaching me.

She folds her arms across her chest; she is in big sister, protective mode. Dom looks at me with dark brown intense eyes. Looking at wide 3-inch-wide gold cuff bracelet with amethyst colors Swarovski crystals dusting over it, I answer her.

"Adam says I am overworked so for him to renew my contract I must take a vacation."

"Miss. Joy," Dominique asks.

"My brother won't let me bring her," I replied.

Dominique laughs.

"Rome is nice," she mused over the idea. "When do we leave?"

"How soon can you go?" I asks.

Dominique looks back at her assistant. Linda shrugs her shoulders and chuckles. I don't wait for an answer from Dominique, I know she is going to go. Slowly, I walk around the boutique looking at the clothes.

"I'm not letting you go to Rome wearing all black," Dominique said, slowly following me around.

I cut my eyes at her being coy.

"I'm the client," I tease.

I pulled a sheer black long off the shoulder toga.

"With that cuff, I will kill this outfit!" I said.

Dominique shakes her head with a smile. My smile is a smirk. One of our friendly yet passive-aggressive arguments where we boss each other around, and this time; I won.

"Linda," Dominique calls her assistant.

Linda quickly approaches me and takes the dress and cuff. I continue to look through the clothes.

"Just think, Dom, we can enjoy the city, the art, the writing, the fashion."

"Let me finish taking inventory, and we can plan," Dominique said, smiling.

Suddenly, I am very excited about the trip. Maybe on this trip, I can write my Gatsby. I would be in a romantic city, and that is something to write about.

While Dominique finished her inventory, I continued to look through her clothes. I see Tommy standing by the window.

*I'm not allowed to write, I said with sarcasm.*

Tommy laughs at me.

*Don't laugh at me! Because of you, I am on creative probation!*

*Me,*

*Yes, you, I still don't have my Gatsby, Adam won't renew my contract until I have a vacation because apparently, I am overworked or stressed or whatever,*

*August, I'm not the cause-* he defends himself.

*You're my muse! You're supposed to inspire me to write my Gatsby.*

Tommy laughs at me and then focuses his attention on the view outside the window. Now, I'm mad, he is not taking me seriously. I approached him.

*Don't laugh, this is serious!*

He looks at me with soft eyes. I can't tell if he was feeling sorry for me or if he understood my creative pain.

*Tonight, you'll help me, I request.*

*How,*

*Take me to Gatsby! We can read the book and see what Fitzgerald did to get the magic of Gatsby and then with my work, I can have that similar magic. Rome, you'll come with me to Rome. Part of Gatsby's magic is location, New York, in the 1920's, the roaring twenties. In the city of prestige, promises, and culture, the Jazz Age. The Harlem Renaissance-,*

*That's wasn't Gatsby,* implied Tommy.

*No, but the culture of the Harlem Renaissance was epic. So much culture came out of New York. I need culture in my work, artistic expression. I am standing in a fashion's boutique. I am surrounded by expression. I need that Gatsby magic,*

"You know," I said to Dominique, "Rome that's Gatsby like. Gatsby is set in the romantic escapade of the 1920's. I need to work on an escapade."

Dominique and I are on our way to her travel agent to book the trip to Rome. As we ride in the taxi, my mind thinks of Janet Jackson's song *Escapade*, she runs off to a romantic rendezvous with a handsome man.

"August," Dominique said.

I looked to her I didn't realize that I had been singing out. She laughs at me.

"Girl, let Janet sing that." She jokes.

"Come on baby, let's get away...," I sing louder.

"Ooooh," she sings and dances in the back seat.

"Let's save your troubles for another day," I sing,
"Ooooh,"

"Come go with me, we got it made...,"

"Let me take you on an escapade," I sang.

"Escapade," the taxi driver sang.

Dominique and I laugh at him. He laughs and continues to sing along.

"We'll have a good time..., I sing.

"Escapade," Cabbie and Dominique sings,

"Leave your worries behind,"

"Escapade,"

"You will be mine...,"

"Escapade,"

I let out a loud yelp. Together we all laugh at our silliness. I didn't care how we sounded, singing off-key. And at that moment, everything changes, my scenery before me is different. It is evening at least seven pm. I look at myself. I am no longer wearing a pair of black Capri pants with a black tank, but I am wearing a black dress, sequined flapper, and my hair is slick back with waves and curls along my edges like the legendary Josephine Baker's hair due called the Baker Fix. I look at my hands, and my nails are painted red.

*When did I get fingernails?*

I turned to look at Dominique, and she wore a gold flapper's dress, her hair cut in a Bob hairstyle, and her lips are bright red.

*THE JAZZ AGE, TOMMY*, I exclaim to myself. *Gatsby!*

The streets looked like old Manhattan.

*August, this is your New York.* I hear Tommy say.

I could hear Tommy, but I can't see him, he's not in the cab.

*Tommy, I'm from Pittsburgh.*

We come to a stop light, I look out the window and see F. Scott Fitzgerald, the F. Scott Fitzgerald.

"It's him, it's him!" I exclaim.

"Who?" I hear Dominique say.

I caught myself. I bring myself into reality. I grin.

"Sorry girl, I thought I saw Idris Elba."

I sit back in the seat. Dominique sighs. I take a deep breath as I listen to the music playing from the cab's radio, jazz music. I grin, the Jazz Age. I close my eyes and put myself back into my fantasy. Dominique and I are going to hear some music. I look out the window and see a young couple meeting on the corner. A handsome white male in his early twenties, hazel-colored eyes that were both endearing and welcoming. He is a musician, a composer, who doesn't want to work in his father's hardware store, but he wants to play in the big band. His name was; Tommy,

*Tommy? I play in the big band.* My Tommy ask.

*No her Tommy is a musician, he plays piano, and the Duke is playing here, tonight. Tommy doesn't live far from here, so he comes to hear him play, enjoy some good music with friends.*

*Who's she?*

*Madeline,* I answer.

Tommy is waiting for his friend Madeline; Miss. Maddie is what he calls her.

*What's the connection?* Tommy asked.

*Madeline works for Tommy's family as their maid in Long Island. His parents would never approve of them socializing, so they met here in Manhattan.*

*I take it that Madeline is colored; African-American.* Tommy said to me.

I nodded my head.

*Two friends who enjoyed each other's company. Not as taboo as it is down south, but something that was not done as freely as you and me.* I said.

*But with certain kinds of people who have their particular type of views.*

I nodded my head. I thought about Gatsby again. Fitzgerald chased the concept of the American Dream, as a writer, that is not my quest. My characters are not in need of material wealth- well *The Beautiful Ones* were they were cutthroat, Jay Gatsby style. With Beef, Joey didn't necessarily want money, just revenge, and Jerica, she just had an usually gift.

*What about the other books?* Tommy asks.

*My characters had emotional turmoil.*

*What's your American Dream?* Tommy asks.

As I open my mouth, I hear someone call my name.

"August!"- I hear my name called.

Suddenly the scenery changes back to New York; my time. I look around at Dominique is sitting beside me staring. I look at my surroundings and see that she and I are at a traveling agency. I had blacked out, I mean totally blacked out. My last memory of her and I and the cap driver singing *Escapade.* I take a deep breath feeling extremely repentant of losing touch of reality. I thought I could handle this- I did the other night at the book party; how did I lose it now?

"I'm sorry, I blacked out for a moment," I said near tears,

I quickly stood up.

"I have to go, D, book whatever, okay, call me tonight with the details."

"Aug-," Dominique said somewhat irritated yet concerned.

I quickly pulled my wallet out and grabbed my credit card. Dominique stands up.

"Excuse us-," she told the travel agent. Dominique pulls me aside. I sigh fearing that I was going to be scolded. I gave her my American Express.

"D, just book the trip, two weeks, flight, everything. I have to run,"

"Where are you going, and what is happening with you?"

"I have to go," I snapped.

I quickly ran out of the travel agency leaving Dominique behind with my credit card. I flag down a taxi.

"Kirby Howard," I said to the driver.

Miles may know how I can obtain my Gatsby. He knows literature. As a matter of fact, he said that he likes The Great Gatsby. He said that he likes my work, he can tell me what I need to do to get Gatsby Greatness.

As I ride the back of the taxi to Kirby Howard, I think about Jay Gatsby; about what he wanted; Daisy. He wanted Daisy. Why? Because of love. There was something lovely and charming about her, when they dated, he could not provide for her in the manner that she has become accustomed. However, as a rich man that knew that she was married, he hoped that she would see his greatness; the splendor that he had created for her and she would want him. What is the one thing that I want? To write that one great American novel. The novel that will stamp me as one of the great American writers. Daisy was unattainable because she was married and the strategies that he chose to win her heart was immoral. What are my strategies? Hallucinating the image of a man thinking that he will enhance my imagination. Is that immoral?

I sit back in the seat of the cab looking at the surroundings, thinking about Gatsby. I loved *The Great Gatsby* for the intrigued, for the cunning, for the love affair, I love Jay Gatsby not for his wealth but for his freedom to be Jay Gatsby. I love the mystery of him. He didn't have to attend his parties, because he was Jay Gatsby.

**I ARRIVE AT *KIRBY*** *Howard* and quickly walk to the reception desk. The pretty receptionist smiles at me, before I could speak, Miles comes from the hallway.

"August,"

I quickly turned around and see him. I suddenly become light-headed, why who knows?

"Are you okay," he asks, approaching me.

Suddenly, I feel ridiculous being here. Why would he care about my quest? What can he contribute? I am embarrassed.

"Come inside," he said to me. "Monica, hold my calls."

I follow Miles into his office.

"I called you to see if you wanted lunch," he said.

I pulled my cell phone out of my pocket and saw there is a missed call. Looking at the time, it was during my *Escapade* sing-a-long.

I don't reply. My silence is alarming.

"What's the matter?" he asks.

I take in a deep breath, he approaches me,

"You're flushed,"

I slowly exhale.

"Sorry, I missed your call, my phone was on silent." I fibbed.

The truth is, with Dom's, the cab driver and me singing, we drowned out the sound of my phone. Miles grins.

"Lunch is cool, but may I ask you something," I ask.

He nods his head indicating for me to continue.

"Your work, it's a matter of opinion, yes?"

"Somewhat, I have facts to stand on,"

"What qualifies a Gatsby?"

"A Gatsby," he asked.

I nodded. Miles look befuddled. I sighed. I was now more embarrassed than before.

"I have too much time on my hands," I murmured.

I made an attempted to leave, but Miles stop me. He looks over me, he blue eyes are intense. He is trying to read me. Considering that he is a guru of Literature, I know that he can read me easily. I take a deep breath.

"You have writers' block?" he asks.

"No," I chuckle. "I want Gatsby greatness,"

Again, he has a befuddled look. I take a deep breath.

"I want to write a great American novel, something that equals to *The Great Gatsby*."

"August, you have people who want to make your book into a movie before the book is released." Miles chuckles.

"But is it Gatsby Greatness?" I ask.

"Do any of your characters come from the bottom and now live a life of luxury?"

I think of them all. All of my books, all of my characters.

"August, some of your characters come from the emotional bottom, and they live the life of eternal blissfulness. With Gatsby, it was the money and what he can do with money. He brought his image, with your characters their image is not brought."

"*The Great Gatsby* was one of a kind. Mark Twain, he was a rebel." I said.

Miles laugh. I laugh too.

"Mark Twain did do his own thing," I said. "You see what I mean. I want to be known, by that one book. Michael Jordan, number twenty-three. Michael Jackson has the *Thriller* album."

"Michael Jackson was not happy with the *Off the Wall* album. He kept pushing and pushing himself. So he focused, and *The Thriller* album was born. That album is still the number one album of all time. Plus, *The Great Gatsby* wasn't a masterpiece until after he died, babe, it was the new generation that loved him and wanted him.

They saw the opulence; they saw the hope. Your generation already see you."

I look away and focus my attention on the view from the window.

"August," said my name softly.

I shift my eyes to face him.

"Want to have dinner tonight,"

I take in a deep breath and then again look away.

"I can't," I look back at him. "The past couple of days my schedule has been hectic, and I haven't spent much time with Joy."

Miles nods his head understanding.

"I'm going to Rome in a few days for a few weeks."

"What's in Rome?" Miles asked. "Another book tour?"

"No," I answered. "Adam said that I need a vacation. I wanted to go to Rome, so," I trailed off.

"Rome," he said. "I've always wanted to go to Rome myself. Study some ancient Roman writers, like, Galan, Ovid, Marcus Aurelius. To see the Vatican Museum, Sistine Chapel, Raphael Rooms."

"What's stopping you?" I ask.

"Rome is not a spontaneous trip, it requires planning, packing, someone to get your mail, water your plants-,"

Suddenly I imagine Miles in Rome, wearing a light blue button-up short sleeve shirt, a pair of khaki pants and black sandals. He also would have some kind of handcraft bracelet on his wrist, and he would be carrying a journal in one arm, and the other arm would be around me. Seeing this vision causes chills to go through my spin, but the more I look at him, the more I want it to be a reality. We would be walking among The Ruins, sightseeing, enjoying the historical culture.

"Come to Rome with me," I requested suddenly, surprising myself.

"What?"

Quickly, I think about what I said. The idea of him and me is making my stomach flip with a feeling that tickles me, like butterflies.

"Rome, come with me," I say again.

Suddenly Janet Jackson's *Escapade* plays in my head again. I grin slightly and pray that he finds me endearing. However, the idea of rejection is causing that butterfly feeling to now become unnerving so quickly I inform him.

"My friend Dominique King is going." I quickly said.

"It's like a girlfriends' trip," Miles says. "I be a third wheel,"

"No," I said, getting hypnotized in his eyes.

I shake my head trying to break the spell. I take a deep breath and slowly exhale.

"Then again, there are some sights I would like to see under the Roman moon," Miles said to me, his looking at me softly.

I grin as Miles smiles at me. He moves closer to me. I can feel my body wanting to hug him, wanting him to hold me. Without thinking, slowly, I move closer to him and inhale in his cologne.

My cell phone rings I sigh. I see that it is Dominique said.

"Hello," I answer.

"You have much explaining to do." she says harshly.

"Did you book the trip?" I ask.

"No,"

"Why not,"

"Because you are goofy, what is going on with you and where are you at?"

"I'm inviting a friend," I informed her.

"Who,"

"Miles Palmer," I answered.

Dominique remains quiet. I could tell that she is smiling. I take a deep breath, but before I can begin to utter an explanation, she sings:

"On an Escapade baby!"

I hung up the phone. I look at Miles,

"I'm hungry," I say quickly, trying to dismiss Dominique comment.

"I know a good Deli," I nod. "Okay, let me settle up a few things here, and I can take you."

"All right,"


**WE SIT IN A DELI** waiting for our lunch. As I sip my ice water and Miles sips his fruit punch, he asks me about Joy.

"Your face lights up when one mentions her name," he says.

I nodded my head.

"Joy is my existence," I say smiling, "Every mother thinks their child is kind of wonderful, but my Joy, she the epitome of amazing. When she looks at me with her brown eyes, big doe-like eyes, it's like she loves me and only me. I am the best mommy in the world, in spite of all my flaws. When she laughs, it's not that cute little girl, but this laugh that is straight from the gut. It's contagious, and when she smiles, the whole room lights up. There is no sun if my Joy is not smiling. I am blessed to have her in my life."

"Would you ever consider having more children?" Miles asks.

"You know, what I never really, well, -,"

"August, it's a yes or no answer," Miles said with a chuckle.

"I know, I know," I answered laughing. "But okay, when I first got married, yeah, I wanted a bunch of babies, ya know, but when I got pregnant with Joy, she was the only positive thing in my marriage. My marriage was very turbulent, stressful,"

"Abusive," Miles said.

I look away.

"August, talk to me," he coaxes in a soft tone.

Only my brother know about the details in my marriage, my friends here New York, know that I had a bad marriage, but the full details they know nothing about.

"August, I'm sorry," Miles said.

"I put the past behind me. I can't talk about it without speaking badly about him, and regardless he is still Joy's father. However, I have considered more children but not with Joy's father."

"Would you remarry?"

I shrug my shoulders,

"One bad apple doesn't ruin the bunch," I reply.

"Okay," he grins.

The waiter brings our food. We ate for a moment and then continued to talk.

"When did you fall in love with literature, when you read *The Great Gatsby?*

I shake my head no and sip my ice water. Miles looks at me shocked by response.

"Toni Morrison's *The Bluest Eyes*," I answer. "I read that when I was a kid, a kid, and was like wow. I read all the heavyweights, Mark Twain, William Faulkner, Steinbeck, J. D. Salinger. Even the heavy hitters of today, Grisham, Patterson, I even read that Twilight Saga,"

"Twilight?" he asked with a chuckle. "Twilight, Hunger Games, Fifty Shades,"

I nodded my head,

"Those are actually good books," I tell him.

"What qualifies a good book?"

"When the reader is actually right there, I mean there, not just the character but the reader also."

"A great novel is when the author's concept captures the spirit of life," Miles said to me.

I wonder if I captured the spirit of life with my characters. Did my characters capture the spirit of life? Joey plotting revenge on Coltogirone, and *The Beautiful Ones* did whatever they wanted to do. And Jerica's Story, she seems to be free. But still I wondered, did I capture the spirit of life?

Dominique booked the trip to Rome. We, including Miles, are set to leave in a week that gives me enough time to spend my time with Joy. During the week, I was summoned to watch every Sponge Bob cartoon for the next week, to watch every Teen Nick Program, and to eat Italian Ice in every flavor. We have plans to go to the amusement park.

**DO YOU THINK THAT,** I'll find Gatsby in Rome, I ask Tommy
The night before I am to leave for my trip. He stands in my room looking out of the window. I sit in my bed while Joy sleeps peacefully beside me. I climb out of bed and approach him. Together, we look outside. Tommy put his arms around my shoulders then rests his head against mine.

*August, he says in a soft tone. Does it bother you that we haven't met?*

*No, I answer, staring at the moon, What if I meet you and you're a prick,*

Tommy chuckled and then affectionately tightened his grip around me.

*This fantasy is sufficient for you?*

*Yeah, but you know what's weird? I asked looking at* him.

*Hmm,*

*You don't do what I say or what I want, I said.*

*What?*

*In a fantasy, it is supposed to go according to whoever is having the fantasy. In a romantic fantasy, I am the fair maiden who is being wooed by the handsome prince. In a heroic epic, I am the heroine in a mighty battle,*

*Do you win? Tommy asks.*

*Of course, I win, I answered almost insulted.*

I back away from him and strut around my room like a proud peacock.

*I am a mighty warrior, a soldier of supremacy. I state.*

Tommy laughs at me. I turned around to face him, and then I approached him. I look at him hard in the eyes. I wonder why I could feel him whenever he is in my arms or me in his. Tommy nods his head towards my bed. I look and saw that a little boy in the bed instead of Joy. I look back at Tommy.

*Who's child?* I ask.

I heard a lot of commotion coming from outside of my room. I walk to see what the noise is about, and I see a woman. A pretty woman with flawless brown skin, she wears purple eyeshadow and has a sheet wrapped around her. There is a gentleman holding her close. He is not appropriately dressed as if he dressed quickly.

"Maddie, I'm sorry," she says smiling at me.

She looks at the gentleman,

"Enough, I will see you next week," she says, smiling at him

Reluctantly the man backs away, quickly glances at me and then quickly walks downstairs. Immediately, I walk to the edge of the stairs. I look back at the woman.

"I can't stand when they think they in love." She comments. "Maddie Baby, what's the matter?"

*Why is the woman calling me Maddie?*

"You look confused and lost." She says. "I didn't wake up the prince did I?"

I walk back to doorway of my room, I look in and see Tommy is still there standing by the window and the little boy still sleeps in my bed. The woman manages to peek in and sees the sleeping boy in my bed.

"The prince is asleep, I'm sorry, baby. Carl was the last john for the night."

*John,* I look at Tommy. *Am I in a whorehouse?*

"Ms. Sadie has me working honey," she says.

She pats me gently on my back and walks down the hall. I shake my head trying to wrap my head around what is happening. Carefully, I walk back into my room, not wanting to wake up the little boy; I accost Tommy.

*Your story from last week,* Tommy began. *Remember you were in the cab with Dominique.*

*But I was a pretty girl with the Josephine Baker haircut, not a whore in a whore house, whose baby is that? Where is my baby!*

Tommy takes me by the arms and pulls me to my bedroom mirror. I look in the mirror see a woman that resembles me. She has brown skin, but her eyes are hazel. My hair short in a cute pixie, slick down with a silk scarf wrap around it. I wear a tan colored nightgown.

*But why am I Madeline?*

I look at the baby sleeping soundly in my bed. I sighed.

*How did I get here?* I asked myself.

*I fell in love with frowned upon passion.* I hear a voice.

Quickly I turned around to find the voice but see no one but Tommy and the sleeping baby in bed. I close my eyes and realize that this is my next story. There is a small desk in my bedroom. My laptop sits on it. I opened the laptop and turned it on and began to write. Madeline tells me her story.

We had a common bond, she says to me. The music; jazz. I would clean their home as he played the piano. He loved the Duke. I would hear him sing. He had this suave, charming, demeanor when he played. His voice, his movements were hypnotic. Sometimes I would find myself caught up in the spell of the music and just listen to him sing.

I was his housekeeper, but he says,

"You work for my parents, not me,"

When I came up from Alabama, his parents offered me room and board to keep their home. They lived in Long Island, New York. They had a large house. I did fairly well. I would cook and clean and mend things for Mrs. The Mrs. was a fidget woman. She paid particular attention to detail, always wanting things to be perfect. She was also a proud woman. She thought it high that her husband owned a hardware store.

"We are doing well," she would tell people.

And she took pride in me,

"My girl," I was introduced.

*Her husband: I called him Sir. He didn't speak much. As long as his meals were hot, he was content. After supper, he would say to me,*

"Very fine meal, Madeline,"

"Thank you, Sir,"

Neither of them said much to me except what was needed to be done. It didn't bother me none because I was saving up my money and trying to go to school. I wanted to be a nurse. I had some savings just need a few more extra dollars, and I would be ready for schooling in the fall. On my down time, when allowed, I would listen to their music. I love jazz music.

I didn't meet Tommy right away. He was out of town with friends. I remember meeting him though. I was listening to some jazz music. I was dancing when he caught me. I saw him laughing at me, not in a mocking manner.

"You must be Madeline," he said.

"Yes sir, I am Madeline Harper," I introduced myself.

"You can save the sirs for my father." He told me with a grin. "You can call me Tommy,"

*He extended his hand for me to shake.*

"Your accent is real strong," he said. "Where are you from?"

"Alabama,"

"My mother said that we got a new maid, she didn't mention someone so young,"

"Your folks went to the Bruners. They say I can have the rest of the evening off, but I can prepare you a plate if you like. I made pot roast with potatoes, green beans, and carrots. I also made an apple pie, and there is lemonade."

"I've already eaten Miss. Maddie, but thank you," he told me with a grin.

I grinned back.

"What are you listening to?" he asked me.

"Just old records I brought up from home. Your parents said that it was all right,"

"May I listen with you?" he asked.

I stood shocked. He wasn't supposed to associate with the help. He chuckled at my expression and went to turn the record player on. I watched him as he listened to the music and then he walked to the piano and began to play along with the music.

"You play real good," I told him.

He looked up at me and smiled.

"You go to school for music?" I asked.

"Nope, business. My father wants me to take over his hardware store." He answered. "Tell me, Miss. Maddie, you come all the way up here to be a maid?"

"Oh, no, I want to be a nurse. School starts in the fall. I just need to earn a little extra money to cover my expenses. You play mighty well not work in the profession,"

"I am in a jazz band, me a few of the fellows. We play at small clubs whenever we can get a gig. One day, I'm going to play with the Duke,"

"Duke Ellington?" I asked.

He nodded.

"That be real nice," I encouraged.

"Maybe when you're not working you can come hear us,"

He wasn't like the other gentlemen back home. I wouldn't necessarily call them gentlemen, but Madea always taught me: If you can't say nothing nice, don't say nothing at all. So, I just call them gentlemen, they be gentlemen to someone if not towards me. Even if it was to make pleasant conversation such as:

"How do you do today," or "Looks like the rain may fall,"

They didn't want to be seen talking with a colored woman, especially someone strange looking like me. They say I am strange cause of my eyes,

"You born with the devil in your eyes,"

"Naw, no devil," I tell them. "I take after my great granddaddy, he had light colored eyes,"

"Colored women don't have colored eyes, they're eyes are black like pits,"

I say, "Sorry to be disappointment," but Madea say that I come with these eyes, she say, I saw angels, and that is why my eyes are bright,"

Silly tales is what I say, the truth is, I am the off spring of sharecroppers; secret passion between them and us that is what caused my yellow eyes.

On that night, sitting with Mr. Tommy, there was comfort with him. He didn't seem nervous talking with me, and it didn't seem to bother him that he was smiling at me. I admit I was nervous, in case his parents see our friendly demeanor and question us. I just didn't want any problems.

One particular evening, a Wednesday night when the Mrs., and Sir had stepped out to spend the evening with their friends. I had set aside a plate for Mr. Tommy. As he ate, I went to the kitchen to straighten things up.

"Miss. Maddie," he called out,

I peeked around the wall,

"Come sit down with me,"

"Ah, no, thank you," I objected.

"Come on," he persisted.

"Mr. Tommy, I already eaten," I said replied.

"So, what, and don't call me Mr. Tommy," he said

"What am I supposed to call you then?" I asked bewildered.

"Tommy," he answered.

He sat back in his seat and looked at me with stern eyes.

"I know what it is like down south with that Whites Only, Coloreds Only nonsense, but not here, okay, not with me."

I took a deep breath not knowing how to respond.

"Miss. Maddie, seriously sit down with me." He insisted.

I slowly approached the table and sat down across from him. A moment passed before he spoke.

"How was your day?" he asked.

"Fine," I said still in shocked. "Yours?"

"Good," he replied.

I noticed that he was low on his lemonade.

"Can I get you more to drink," I asked quickly standing up.

He stood up.

"Madeline, seriously, sit down, I can get more lemonade. Would you like some?"

His question caught me off guard. He didn't wait for me to answer. Instead, he went into the kitchen and brought out a pitcher and a glass. I watched as he poured my glass first and then he refilled his.

"Thank you," I finally spoke.

He grinned.

"Ah, how's supper?" I asked.

"Real good, thank you," he answered smiling at me, "tell me something, Miss. Maddie, you're not used to white folk being nice to you, huh?"

I was shocked by his question.

"Where I come from, the help don't socialize with the boss,"

Tommy nodded his head realizing that I was being evasive considering that I didn't want to comment on race.

"Are you off duty?"

"Yes,"

"Okay, technically, you not the help and considering that you work for my parents, you're not my help,"

I chuckled then shook my head. He too laughed.

"I've been told that I am before my time. A social rebel, not following the structure of normal society. I like to go into the city and play music with my friends, color means nothing to me."

I grinned, flattered at his open-mindedness for mankind. I looked at his plate and noticed that he had finished his supper.

"Would you like more," I asked referring to his plate.

"Actually no, but do you have any of your apple pie?"

"I do; would you like me to fix you a slice?" I asked.

Tommy shook his head no,

"Just point to where it is," he said.

Throughout the rest of the evening, Tommy and I talked and laughed, and we listened to jazz.

There was one evening, Tommy came home to invite me to a jazz concert in Manhattan.

"Just say that you're meeting friends," he suggested.

"What friends, I don't have friends," I said to him.

"We're friends," he said to me.

I happened to be scrubbing the kitchen floor. He kneeled down in front of me. We looked at each other for a while, I looked away.

"Maddie, you won't get into trouble, you're not doing anything wrong. It's in the evening, so it's after your work."

I started to scrub again,

"Maddie, come on, the Duke, Count Bassie, Ella, all of the greats. My friends will be there,"

I sighed,

"Okay, but I can make any promises. Who knows what they have planned for me."

Tommy grinned.

Tommy's parents gave me the evening off. He told me where to meet him in Manhattan.

I stopped writing. I am at the part where I was, and I thought I saw F. Scott Fitzgerald in their New York.

*Keep going August.* Tommy: my Tommy encouraged.

During the evening, the big band roared, and we all danced, and for the first time since I've been in New York, I felt alive. I was not looked upon as the hired help, but as Tommy's friend. I was at the table, and I was being served dinner.

Tommy's friends were extremely lovely. Some of his friends were radicals, fighting for some cause. Some of them were idealists, chasing after the big dream and then there were some that came out like me to hear some good jazz. I watched Tommy's face lit up when the Duke took the stage. It was like he was in his own world; it made my heart swell with joy when he smiled. And when it looked like the Duke was looking at Tommy, he almost exploded.

Dancing on the dance floor, I was beyond exciting. I found myself dancing with Tommy. He was surprisingly a good dancer. It didn't seem awkward to those standing by or those dancing among us, and no one cared who danced with whom, they just wanted to dance to the music.

"Are you glad that you came," Tommy asked me.

We had stepped outside for some fresh air.

"Yes, I am, thank you for inviting me," I answered him smiling.

"I told you, Miss. Maddie," he said as he cradled my chin.

"Miss. Maddie," I said softly. "Why is it that you can call me Miss. Maddie, and I can't call you Mr. Tommy?"

Tommy looked at me with tender eyes, then he smiled this smile that I was not familiar with from him, it was flirtatious and endearing.

"You always smile when I call you Miss. Maddie. I like to see you smile."

I suddenly grew nervous and then looked away.

"Did I say something wrong?" he asked.

"No," I said. "You just have a way with words,"

A Moment passed between us,

"I like you, Ms. Maddie," he confessed. "I think you're classy, amazing, and beautiful. I don't care about your color, I don't care about-,"

"Tommy," I interrupted.

"Madeline, I don't care about what my family says, about what society says. I know that I think about you all the time, I can't wait to see you,"

I didn't know what to say. I like Tommy, he was sweet and kind. He made me laugh, and whenever I was around him, I didn't feel like his maid. But being with him was wrong and for so many reasons, but as I looked at him, there was a sense of affection towards him. Tommy leaned forward towards me, but just then one of his friends came outside to join us.

"Miss. Maddie would like me to take you home." He offered me.

"Maddie lives close to me, I can take her home." Tommy said quickly.

"All right, good night," his friend said to both of us.

We all bid each other good night.

"Tommy, what are your parents goin' say when they see us coming in together,"

"I will handle things," he said.

"August," I hear someone say.

I shake my head; I don't want to leave. I am comfortable being Maddie. I am comfortable with Tommy; her Tommy.

"August," I hear my name again.

"What time did she go to bed last night?" asked a familiar voice.

"Your guess is as good as mine," someone answered.

"August, come on,"

I feel tugging and pulling. I finally open up my eyes. I see my brother, Joy and Dominique staring at me. I sit up and see Tommy; my Tommy sitting on the edge of my bed.

"You're going to miss your flight," X., informed.

I can't cancel this trip, but right now I need to know what Madeline did considering Tommy. Dating him was unthinkable especially considering that she was his maid. A colored country bumpkin from the south dating a white city slicker was taboo. Where would they live? Who would they associate with? Or would they just limit their living to the north? Considering Tommy's dreams of being a musician that would involve him touring.

**AS I GET MYSELF** together, I think more about Maddie. She liked Tommy. When she thought about him, she got butterflies in her stomach. She smiled, but her job was important, nursing school was important. Madeline began to avoid him. The nights where she usually would see him, she hid in her room. Tommy would come home, and there was no sound of jazz music filling the air.

One day, when Tommy knew that his parents were not around, he made a point to speak with Madeline. He found her in the backyard hanging up the linen. He slowly approached her. He startled Madeline when she turned around and saw him standing before her.

"Good afternoon, Miss. Maddie," he said to her sweetly.

"Mr. Tommy, you scared the living daylights out of me," she replied catching her breath.

"So formal," he replied.

Madeline quickly looked away.

"Madeline,"

He reached out to grab her.

"We're not friends anymore?" he asked in a solemn manner.

His question broke her heart.

*August, what's going on?* Tommy, my Tommy asked.

I double checked my luggage while Joy sang a song from the Cheetah Girls 2 soundtrack, the song *Strut*. I took a moment to watch her do the choreography with the girls.

*You gotta strut like you mean it,*
*Free your mind*
*It's not enough just to dream it*
*Come on, come on, get up*
*When you feel it, it's your chance to shine*
*Strut like you mean it,*
*Come on, come on, yeah*

"August, do you have enough journals?" Dominique asks with sarcasm, looking through my carry-on bag.

I don't answer. I just watched Joy do a shimmy with Raven-Symone. Then I walk into the kitchen, and the scenery change to the Mr. and Mrs.'s kitchen. I saw Tommy; Madeline's Tommy. He followed her from the backyard. I watch her wash the dishes as Tommy attempts to plea with her for her heart. Now, instead of her telling me the story, I am now watching their story. I'm in the scene, watching and observing everything; and now my story shifts from past tense to present tense.

"Of course, we're friends," she answers. "but you are putting me in a difficult position. If your parents find out how you feel about me, I can lose my job! I will have to move back home and there ain't nothing there for me."

"Maddie, I can't hide my feelings for you. What if you work someplace else,"

"What?" Madeline asked appalled.

"Madeline, this is not the only job in New York. Maybe you can-,"

"I am not going to risk messing something up," Madeline exclaims. "Your folks have been real good to me. I just want to go to school and be done with everything,"

"Okay, okay," Tommy says surrendering. "I am being real selfish,"

He leans against the sink. For a moment, they looked at each other until she broke, she looks away bashfully.

"I've missed you," he finally speaks.

Tommy moves in close to her, gently he takes her arms and pulls her close to him, and then he takes his hands and cradles her face into his palms. Her moon shaped eyes cause him to smile. He leans forward and kisses her.

"Bye Mommy, I love you," Joy said wrapping her arms around my neck.

We give each other Eskimo kisses.

"Want me to call you in the mornings like last time?"

"Every morning," I said to her, "You know I can't start the day without my Joy."

Joy giggles.

"Next time, me and you will go away. Can we go to Barcelona like the Cheetah Girls?" she asks with her eyes wide with hope and anticipation.

I nodded my head,

"We can go anywhere you want to go."

She wraps her arms around me and Eskimo kisses me again. The cab honks its honks its horn loudly. Immediately Xavier begins to take our luggage to the cab.

"Bye Miss. Joy," Dominique said Joy.

Joy waves at Dominque and then Dominique waves at my brother.

**"SO, MS. SCHOFIELD," DOMINIQUE** begins. "Are you excited about your little escapade?"

"What?" I ask checking my email through my phone.

"Miles Palmer," she says with a smile.

"It's not an escapade," I said trying to be evasive.

"August, you invited a man on a vacation," Dominique said, smiling. "Why are you fighting your emotions?"

"I'm not fighting anything, I'm just saying, I am not anticipating going over to Rome for sex, I can have sex here. I just want to spend time with Miles; that's all,"

"Does he like you?"

"He says he does," I answer.

Dominique grins. "Have you guys been out?"

"We had lunch a few times," I answer.

She grins as I look out of the window.

"Dom, don't make a big deal out of this. I don't know what this is."

"You don't know what this is?" Dominique scoffs. "August, you like him. Just say it, admit it. He likes you too because he is going to Rome with you."

"Okay," I said with a sigh.

Dominique takes my hand.

"Go with the flow," she says. "Do what you want to do. You want to like him, then like him. Have fun and don't worry about anyone."

"Okay," I say with a grin.

**WE ARRIVE AT THE** airport to meet Miles and one of his friends, Rodney, waiting. He smiles as we approach. He greets me with a hug and shakes Dominique's hands and introduces us to his staff. Our flight is not scheduled to leave for an hour. As everyone sits down to make idle chit-chat, Miles leads me to a small and secluded corner.

"I haven't heard much from you." He says, smiling. "How are you?"

"Good," I answered.

"I am, ah, looking forward to this trip," he says, appearing to be nervous, which is now making me nervous.

Then I realized that Miles standing too close as if we were an actual couple. Is this how close we stood in his office? What kind of adventures did he anticipate while in Rome? I look back at Dominique; she is talking with Rodney.

"I can't wait to see the Sistine," Miles says to me.

I grin. Tommy; both Tommys are standing behind me, one on my left and one on my right. Her Tommy whispers:

"My parents are going away for the weekend,"

A chill goes through me causing me to shiver.

"You okay?" Miles asks

"Yeah," I answered taking a deep breath. "Just had a chill,"

Miles grins and then he takes his hands and rubs them up and down my arms.

Miles and I sit together on the plane. He talks endlessly about something, but I smile pretending that I am listening inventively, but I kept zoning out of reality.

Tommy has been courting Madeline secretly for three weeks. The nights when he doesn't see her, he would slip a love note in her door and the nights when they were together, they would listen to jazz music, sit and talk. He would tell Madeline about his dreams of being a successful jazz musician, his ultimate dream of playing with the Duke.

Tommy tries to plan and romantic weekend. His parents are going to Buffalo, New York for a friend's wedding. Tommy finds Madeline in the kitchen. He sneaks behind her and steals a kiss.

"Stop," she says cautiously, "Your momma is right upstairs."

He playfully makes a face as he tickles her and then pulled her into his arms. She tries to resist, but eventually, she gives up and wraps her arms around his shoulders and for a moment they kiss each other passionately.

"My parents are going away for the weekend," he says.

Madeline grins, and she removes herself from his arms. She thinks she hears his mother stirring. Madeline continues to prepare dinner while Tommy whispers to her.

"We can really be together," he suggests. "All day, all evening. We can even go to the jazz lounge," Madeline grinned. "That be nice, huh?"

"What if I have work?"

"Doing what?" he asks.

"I don't know,"

"Maddie, you and me, no one else. We stay here if it makes you feel better. You, me, and jazz,"

**"YOU, ME, AND ROME."** Miles said.

A moment passes, "August,"

"Yes," I answer.

"What's the matter, you seem distant,"

I take a deep breath.

"I'm sorry," I say.

He waits for me to explain myself.

"I've just have a lot on my mind," I confess.

He looks almost discouraged as if I something wrong.

"Is everything all right,"

"Yeah, just ah, brainstorming some ideas on a new book,"

"Oh," he said seeming interested. "Is there a block?"

"No," I said. "Everything is coming along all right, I just-,"

"Want to write," he said.

I nodded my head casually then shrugged my shoulders. I look at Dominique who is engaging in deep conversation with Rodney. Dominique notices me watching her. She is so cool when she talks with men. Me, I am a nervous wreck. She smiles at me and then sits up and looks at both Miles and me.

"August is on this quest to write a great American novel," Dominique says to Miles, teasing me.

"Dom," I say shooting her a look.

"Yeah, I know," Miles says with a chuckle.

"She goes off into another world and ignores, you know real reclusive, but somehow you managed to bring my baby out, and now we're off to Rome."

I watch as Dominique talks to Miles as if I am not here.

"The article you did on August is fascinating. If I didn't know August myself, I would like to,"

"You talk as if August Schofield is complicated," Miles says.

"Stick around, and you'll see," she says with a wink.

Miles grin and then looks at me.

I grab my journal from my carry-on and begin to write with hopes that Miles and Dominique get the hint to leave me alone.

I lie in Tommy's arms. He is sound asleep. I don't want this weekend; our weekend to end. He promised romance. After his parents left for their weekend trip, Tommy and I spent every moment together. We ate dinner by candlelight; he wouldn't let me cook. It was sweet to watch him try to cook. However, after a few failed attempts, I did prepare our meals. Tommy filled the rooms with flowers. He got gardenias, just like the kind that Billie Holiday wears, and he put them in my hair.

"You ever see Lady Day sing?" he asked me one night.

We were dancing. I shook my head no.

"She is amazing," he said.

Listening to the jazz and dancing slowly, I felt safe in his arms. I felt beautiful. For the first time, I didn't think about his parents or work. I just imagined him and me, together. Tommy and Maddie, Madeline and Thomas.

"Miss. Maddie, I love you," he whispered.

I look at him.

"I do,"

I wake up to him playing the piano. I take a bath and quickly dress and go downstairs to greet him.

"Why didn't you wake me," I said sitting next to him on the piano.

"You looked so peaceful, I didn't want to wake you,"

"Would you like some breakfast," I ask standing up.

"I had some toast," he answers.

"That's not breakfast," I laughed. "Let me fix you something."

"No working, we're on vacation," he said to me.

"I don't see no harm in preparing you something to eat," I said to him.

"No harm," he says softly.

He looks at me, leans forward and kisses me.

"I love you," I look away. "It's okay if you don'-,"

"No, I do," I said, looking at him. "I love you,"

We sat still for a moment, our heads pressed together, telling each other that we love each other. I hear his stomach growl.

I laugh.

"Let's me fix you breakfast,"

"Okay, Miss. Maddie," he surrenders sweetly.

Together Tommy and I go to the kitchen. I prepared breakfast for us. As I scrambled his eggs, I can't believe how much I am in love with him. Is it possible to love someone that much, that fast? Am I just caught up in the spell of this weekend? Soon his parents will return, and I will go back to being the hired help.

Tommy and I arrived in Manhattan. He booked a room for just the two of us. As we lay under the cover, he begins to share some news with me.

"Someone noticed my friends and me one day at the club playing,"

"Really?"

"Yeah, and he said that he wants us to play for them for a few of their concerts."

"Tommy, that's awesome," I exclaim, sitting up. "What did your folks say?"

"I haven't told them yet," he said. "I wanted to tell you first,"

Tommy sits up.

"If he likes us, we will leave in a week and go to Europe."

I don't respond.

I take a deep breath. I look at him for a moment and then climb out of bed.

"We better get back," I said reaching for my clothes,

"Maddie,"

"I have a lot to do in the morning," I said beginning to get dressed.

"Maddie," he calls for me again.

Tommy climbs out of bed and quickly reaches for me.

"You don't owe me anything," I say quickly. "I enjoyed us,"

"Madeline, will you stop," he said. "Listen to me. I want you to come with me."

"No," I said.

"Why not?"

"I don't belong on the road," I told him. "I'm a housekeeper, I am going to school for nursing. Plus, what it look like with me on your arm."

"Madeline, why is it always about color with you,"

I turned my back to him. I can't understand how he ignores what society says. Why does he feels that we can honestly live in a world of racial harmony.

"Madeline, we'll be playing in Europe. Over there, no one cares about race. You can live and do what you want."

"I'm going to school," I snap.

I turned around to face him.

"I want to go to school."

"Maddie,"

"Tommy, schooling is important to me, I'll be the first in my family to go,"

He sighs.

"Okay," he said.

"Go on the road," I said as tears well up in my eyes.

There is a lump in my throat,

"You don't owe me anything-,"

"Stop saying that," he said. "Maddie, I love you; I will only be gone for a couple of weeks when I come back, and we'll get married."

"Marriage, we ain't never talked about marriage before,"

"We will get married. I will take care of you. You won't have to work for my parents, and you can go to school."

He doesn't wait for an answer. Tommy wraps his arms around me.

"Wait for me," he says.

He left to go play with his big band. I am lonely and miserable. I miss him so much. Tommy wrote to me, and I have written back, but it is not the same. I don't want him by mail. I want him with me. Playing with me; teasing me. We would sneak kisses when we thought no one was looking. I miss him so much. I wonder if he thinks of me when he is playing. Does he miss kissing me underneath the stars? I know that there are other women around, but do they matter? He said that he loved me.

"August," someone calls my name.

I shake my head not wanting to come out not wanting to leave The Land of Aug.

The letters stop coming as often as they once did. My heart is breaking. I hear it said that someone can die of a broken heart, but I never thought of it to be true, but my body is taken the toll of my heartbreak. I am tired, and my headaches. I am so emotional that the sight of food made me sick. Tommy's parents recommended that I go see a doctor.

Pregnant was my diagnosis, not lovesickness. I don't want to be pregnant. What about nursing school?

What about my job? As I sit alone in my room, I know that I can't stay with Tommy's parents; not being pregnant. What if the baby looks like Tommy? After I arrived home, Mr. and Mrs. asked me if everything was all right with the doctors. I told them yes; it is just a common cold. I have to wait until they are both gone to look for new employment.

I watch as the gentlemen walk down the steps followed by the pretty woman. I pretend that I am not offended by the sight as I speak to Miss. Sadie about my new employment.

"I can use a maid, business is real heavy," Miss. Sadie told me. "I will need you to run the women's bath, clean up their rooms, and keep the liquor stocked."

I nodded my head.

"When can you start?" Miss. Sadie asks.

"Let me settle business with my current employer, and I can start tomorrow."

"All right,"

So, I told Mr. and Mrs., that my great aunt had taken ill and I will need to care for her.

I felt bad for lying. I left their home crying and emotional not knowing what to do. My dreams of being a nurse were no longer optional.

Working for Miss. Sadie isn't so bad. I basically clean all day. I clean the bedrooms and wash the linen and the ladies' nightwear. I fix everyone's breakfast made lunch and dinner. All of the ladies are nice. When I get a free moment, I sit and listen to Miss. Sadie's records.

Then one day I noticed her watching me.

"You in trouble," she said with a cunning grin.

"No ma'am," I answer, knowing what she meant.

"Who's the daddy?" Miss. Sadie questions.

I look away.

"He don't need to know nothing," I answer.

"I can make some arrangements for you, if you like," Miss. Sadie suggests.

I think for a moment if I get rid of my baby then I reconsider nursing school just enroll for next year. I can save up the money and live on my own. But this baby is Tommy's baby, and even if he doesn't love me anymore, this baby is evident that he loved me once.

"No, ma'am," I told her.

Ms. Sadie approaches me.

"Wha cha goin do wit dat baby?" she asks. "Goin ta be hard raising a baby and keep house. Too many working women here. This ain't no place for children. My johns see you, you scare them away,"

"Leave her alone," said a voice from behind.

A woman walks forward. I watch her hips sway side to side. Her brown face is pretty, and she has red lips to match her red dress.

"You stay out of this Ruthie," Ms. Sadie snaps. "Dis girl is goin ta cost me money,"

"No she ain't!, She ain't even seen. She cleaning, cooking, minding her own business when the baby comes, she can decide on what to do,"

"Who running my house?" Ms. Sadie snaps angrily.

"The best one you got here," Ruthie said putting her hands on her hips. "Plus, she the best house cleaner we had, so back off!"

She gives Miss. Sadie a scornful stare. To my surprise, Miss. Sadie backs down.

"Ain't goin' be no babies in here, once you have dat baby, you out," says walking away.

I look at Ruthie,

"Thank you," I say bashfully.

"You welcome," Ruthie says smiling. "Her bark is worse than her bite."

Ruthie winks a friendly wink at me and walks away. With my hand on my belly, I take a deep breath and continue to clean.

Ruthie has become my friend she has a sweet spirit. She is kind and sweet, not like the other women who are hard, cold and shallow. For the past few months, as my belly grew, she and I would sit on the stoop during the nights when either of us couldn't sleep. She shared with me her dreams and goals, and they were like mine. She had wanted to be a nurse but got sidetracked. When she was a little girl, she was raped; raped to the point of never being able to have children. Although she was devastated, she didn't want to play the victim, and by being a nurse, she could help people. She needed a little money for schooling. She met Ms. Sadie, and the rest is history.

"What's your story?" she asks me one night.

I rubbed my belly as my baby kicked. Most of the women say it's a boy. I'm not sure. It don't matter as long as my baby is healthy.

"Not much of a story," I answer. "Just got caught up in love,"

"He didn't want the baby,"

"No, just ah," I stammered. "our lives would have been complicated."

**"AUGUST," I HEAR MY NAME** "August,"

I sigh wondering who is calling me. I open my eyes and see my friends.

"She does this," Dominique says.

"Does what?" I hear Miles voice.

"She blacks out whenever she writes,"

I look at my surroundings. We are still on the airplane. How long was I out? I looked for Tommy, my Tommy. He is sitting in front of me

I need a break. I tell him.

He shakes his head no.

What did she have? He asks.

I grin and look out of the window.

A boy, Judah, it means praise.

Miss. Sadie is in love with the handsome baby. She plays the surrogate grandma while Madeline did her housework. In fact, all of the ladies love Judah. He was adorable, light brown skin with Madeline's hazel eyes. He has dimples and dark curly jet-black hair.

**"AUGUST, YOU, OKAY?" MILES** asks me in a soft tone.

I look at him. His blue eyes smiling at me.

"Yeah, I'm okay," I said. "I'm sorry if I am distant."

Miles' eyes glanced at the notebook my lap, and then he looks at me.

"Will you be doing this the whole trip?"

I quickly glance at Tommy. He shrugs his shoulders. I look back at Miles.

I feel bad that I have been writing, especially that I invited Miles on this trip but at this moment, I don't want to leave my world. My writing is pulling me strong. Adam told me no writing, but how is that possible?

"Miles would you mind if I complete this thought," I asked hoping not to offend him.

He smiles, takes my hand and kisses it. I smile back.

"I want to know about it later, okay," he says.

I nod my head with a grin and focus my attention on my notes. I can feel Tommy next to me as if he is reading over my shoulder. Madeline and Judah.

Several years have passed. Judah has become a prince to the ladies at Miss. Sadie's. Madeline tries best to shield him from the activities and subject matters of the home. Sometimes Ruthie and Madeline would take Judah to the park to run around and play with the other children.

This particular Saturday afternoon Maddie didn't have time to take him, so Ruthie volunteered. As Judah plays with the other children, Ruthie sits on the bench and watch him. Two men approached the bench. They are young and nice looking. Both dark haired men. One seemed outgoing, he was flashy and charismatic and the other quiet and reserved.

Ruthie smiles as they approach. The loud and flashy one makes the first move.

"Ms. Ruthie, my, my, my, fancy meeting you here," he says smiling.

Ruthie grins

"Paul, how are you,"

"Doing just fine baby, now that I see you,"

"I bet you say that to all the ladies," Ruthie said playing doubtful.

"Awe baby, you know you're my New York girl,"

Paul extends his hand to Ruthie. She takes it, and he pulls her to him, and they share a warm and affectionate embrace.

"I am in town, baby, and I want to see you." He tells her. "Cancel those other johns and book me for the week. I'll pay double."

Ruthie giggles.

"Excuse me, baby, let me introduce my man, Tommy, meet Ruthie, Miss. New York."

Tommy shook her hand politely.

"You have someone classy for my friend," Paul asks.

"Ah, Paul," Tommy interjects. "I don't need-,"

"Be cool, baby," Paul said to Tommy, "Miss Sadie's house is not just your average brothel. Real classy joint. Ruthie will take care of you,"

Ruthie grins at Paul.

"I have to run, but tonight come on through, and bring your friend,"

Ruthie leans in and kisses Paul on the cheek. She calls for Judah. Paul is surprised to see the small child running towards her.

"You didn't get maternal on me," he replied laughing.

"No silly, I'm babysitting for my friend,"

Ruthie blows Paul a kiss and takes Judah by the hand and leaves.

Ruthie peeks her head in Madeline's room. She smiles at her friend who is trying to get Judah to go to sleep.

"You look pretty," Madeline said to Ruthie.

"Thank you, baby," Ruthie said. "Can I borrow your pearl earrings? I want to look real classy for Paul."

Without waiting for an answer and knowing that Madeline will share, Ruthie walks into Madeline's room and to the dresser to get the earrings.

"Paul is the type of man that can make a girl wanna stop trickin'," Ruthie says, as she poses in front of the mirror

"Is that right," Madeline said with a chuckle.

"Yes, he actually treats me like a lady,"

"You are a lady," Madeline said to her.

"Yeah, but with what I do, the fellas get what they want, and that is it. With Paul, he takes me out to dinner, nice places, talks to me, asks me how I feel."

Madeline smiles at her friend. Ruthie looks at Judah.

"Was it like that with Judah's father?"

"Judah's father," Madeline says thinking for a moment, "We lived in a world of possibilities, not in the world of realities."

"So, what he didn't want children?"

Madeline shrugs her shoulders indicating that she doesn't want to talk about him anymore. She looks at her son; their son, sleeping soundly in her bed. A little man, her Prince Judah.

"I have some things I need to finish up downstairs," Madeline says getting up. "Help yourself to anything in the box,'

Madeline goes downstairs to the back room. There is a knock at the door, Miss. Sadie answers it. It is Paul and Tommy. As they step inside, Paul smiles at Miss. Sadie.

"Good evening, Miss. Sadie." Paul said smiling.

"Hi you doin' baby," Miss. Sadie smiles back at Paul.

The two share an affectionate embrace. Miss. Sadie looks at Paul's friend. He seems shy and withdrawn.

"Honey, I have a real nice girl for you," Ms. Sadie says to Tommy.

Tommy grins politely.

"Would two fellas like something to drink?" Miss. Sadie asks, walking into the living room.

"Scotch on the rocks and make his neat," Paul says to Miss. Sadie, following her.

Miss. Sadie nods her head as she walks to the bar. Ruthie comes down the stairs smiling.

"My, my," Paul said smiling at her.

Paul and Ruthie hugged each other, Ruthie then looked at Tommy,

"Franny be down in a minute for you,"

Tommy grins.

"Miss. Sadie, I get the drinks," Ruthie offers.

"All right," Miss. Sadie says looking at Tommy and Paul, "You fellas have a good night,"

"Good night, Miss. Sadie," both Tommy and Paul said.

Miss. Sadie walks away.

"Paul, how is the music going?" Ruthie asks.

"We got some gigs lined up, and we're about to record for a new album," Paul says to her, as she hands him and Tommy their drinks.

"My man here is dangerous on the piano," Paul said pointing to Tommy.

"Is that so?" Ruthie inquires impressed.

Tommy grins modestly.

"He writes music too," Paul boasts.

"I don't know where Franny is," Ruthie said nervously.

Ruthie calls for Madeline.

"Miss. Madeline, you still down here," Ruthie calls out to the back room. "Miss. Maddie,"

Within moments, Madeline comes forward. Tommy looks up and sees her, Madeline. Is this his Madeline?

"Get Franny for me, baby," Ruthie request politely.

"I'm right here," said a voice coming from the steps.

Ruthie looks at Franny.

"Madeline," Tommy says to Madeline.

Madeline focuses her eyes on the person that called her. Tommy. Her heart stops, and she stands still for a moment frozen, not able to believe that Tommy is really in front of her.

"You know Maddie?" Ruthie asks, as Tommy stood up.

He keeps his eyes on Madeline. Then suddenly, Ruthie sees something familiar in Tommy's face. Judah has that face.

"What's going on?" Franny asks.

Ruthie holds her hand up to Franny indicating for her to wait. Franny's eyes look at Paul who slightly shrugs his shoulders.

"Tommy," Paul says.

Slowly, Tommy walks to Madeline. Both of their hearts race rapidly; neither of them don't know if they should embrace each other. Tommy wants to hug her, he missed Madeline.

*Why did you leave?* He wonders.

"Hi," Madeline says, as tears fell from her eyes.

She manages to smile. Tommy almost aggressively grabs her in his arms, Madeline begins to cry.

Ruthie looks at Franny.

"I'll go," Franny says, feeling somewhat irritated.

"Paul, let's leave them alone," Ruthie said.

Paul stands still stunned and confused by the sudden event that took place.

"Paul," Ruthie said.

He finally turns to Ruthie,

"Come on, honey," Paul said to Ruthie.

She holds her hand out for him. He takes her hand, and they leave to go outside.

For a long time, Madeline and Tommy held each other, neither of them wanting to let go. But Tommy does let go, he steps back to look at her face. Then he moves closer, take his thumbs and wipes the tears from her eyes and then kisses her passionately.

"Where have you been?" he asks in a soft tone.

She doesn't answer.

"Madeline please don't tell me you work here,"

She looks away from Tommy,

"Maddie, why?" he asks appalled.

"I'm not one of the girls, I'm their maid," Madeline defends herself.

"Another maid," he scoffs, shaking his head. "Why did you leave?"

"Things got complicated." She begins.

Tommy's eyes question the complication. Madeline takes a deep breath.

"Follow me," she says.

Madeline leads Tommy upstairs to her room. She opens up the door, and together they walk inside. Immediately Tommy's eyes go to the sleeping child. He stands still for a minute; almost frozen. Then Tommy looked at Madeline, his eyes asking the question, her eyes answered her question.

"I saw him today at the park when Paul was talking to Ruthie," Tommy says coolly.

"His name is Judah,"

"Why didn't you tell me?"

"I couldn't," she said. "I mean if your parents have found out. Tommy, I had to go. Your letters, stopped. I assumed you didn't-,"

"I never stopped loving you," he says. "Our schedule was hectic. When I came home and didn't see you. They told me you have moved back home."

Madeline shakes her head,

"No, I had to tell them that when I found out about Judah. So, I move here, been here since. The girls here love him. They fight over him. Tommy, he's a real prince,"

"He can't stay here," Tommy said, looking at Judah.

He looks at Madeline.

"You can't stay here," Tommy grabs her in his arms. "You and our son, we'll be together,"

"August," I hear my name called.

I look up from my journal and see Miles smiling at me. It is time to get off the plane. We are at our layover. I look around confused. I don't remember the stewardess or the pilot telling us to put our seat belts on. I notice that my head is aching. I am tired and hungry.

**WE FIND A PLACE** to eat at the airport. Before we sat down to eat, Dominique and I went to the restroom to freshen up. I fill the sink up with warm water and basically dunk my head in.

"August," she cries out, pulling me from the water.

My head is soaking wet. Luckily, my hair is pulled back into a high bun.

"What is the matter with you?" she admonishes.

I don't answer.

"This book must be good," she replies, as she grabs sheets of paper towels.

I ignore her and dunk my head back into the sink. I hear her call my name again, but I ignore her. The water is reviving me. I come up from the sink feeling somewhat alive. I look at her with my face dripping with water. She shakes her head at me as if she is disappointed in me.

This time, I let her help dry me off.

"You doze off, talking in your sleep," Dominique says drying me off again.

"Are you serious?" I ask.

She nods.

"What was I saying?" I ask.

"Tommy," she answers. "You kept saying Tommy."

"Tommy?"

"Who's Tommy?" Dominique asks.

*Who, which one?* I ask myself.

Considering the overwhelming fatigue, and I have a headache. The Tommy I was calling was probably my Tommy.

"You look drained," Dominique says to me.

"Jet lag," I tell her.

"No, baby, you," she said. "August, I know you're tired and you want to write, but you have to relax, okay. This is what this trip is for you,"

I take a deep breath and nod my head. But I know that I am not done writing. Tommy and Madeline have found each other again. Will they get back together to raise Judah? I can't stop now. I need to know the outcome.

"I can see the way he looks at you," Dominique says.

"Who?" I ask catching my breath.

Dominique begins to massage my shoulders.

"Miles, August," she said with a chuckle. "Whenever he looks at you, he is looking for you, it is so romantic. The Quest for August Schofield,"

"I am so tired," I said to her.

I roll my head around enjoying my massage.

I stand in front of the mirror. She continues to talk,

"Whatever you're looking for, it's right in front of you," Dominique says.

~

**DOMINIQUE AND I REJOIN** our friends. They had already picked out a table. I sit next to Miles. Our table is somewhat secluded.

"You feeling better," Miles asks.

"Yeah," I answer.

The waiter comes and sits down a glass of water. Then he takes our orders. We order the same thing; cheeseburger and fries with a cola.

"Is it always so intense?" Miles asks.

"Is what so intense?"

"You're writing," he says. "It was like your writing had consumed you,"

I nodded my head and stare directly into his eyes.

"It was like you weren't in the room; well on the plane,"

I casually shrugged my shoulders as if it was nothing.

"Did Tommy Gibbs-,"

"Miles," I cut him off.

Miles looks away. I look away. I feel bad that I snapped. I sigh.

"Miles, Tommy Gibbs is off limits," I said to him sternly.

Miles nods his head,

"Okay, I'm sorry,"

I sit back in my seat; the mood has now changed. What is the big secret? I can tell that was what he is thinking, but Tommy belongs to me.

**WE BOARD OUR NEXT** plane, but my demeanor changed. This time, I don't sit with him. I sit in a different seat writing and going over my notes. Miles listens to his iPod. We didn't talk much during dinner. I had wondered if he was mad at me. I invited him to Rome only to Ignore him, so much for my escapade, but I need to write. I can feel Tommy, my Tommy.

"August," Dominique said. "Why are you over here and he's over there?"

"He's mad at me," I answer.

"Why,"

"Because he is getting personal and I snapped,"

"August stop acting stupid." She said sternly. "You're going to make him think you don't like him, I told you that he is looking for you."

"Dominique, I'm writing here," I said.

She shakes her head at me.

"Why are you running?"

"I'm not running, Dom. I invited him, I want to be with him, but I really have to write. My heart, my mind, will not be on him, but on my work."

"Okay, then explain that to him," she said encouraging me.

"Why should I? He's the only that got personal,"

"August go!" she orders me to Miles' corner.

I sat back in my seat and sulk for a moment. I sigh and slowly walk to Miles. He grins when he sees me. He must have been writing because he had his laptop up.

*Why is he allowed to write and not me?*

Rodney grins at me and quickly stands up.

"August, here." He offered me his seat.

I watch as he walks to where Dominique sits, and he sits down beside her.

"May I sit?" I ask.

"Sure," he answers.

As I sat down, I looked at him. His eyes are smiling at me.

"I really don't know what to say," I reply nervously.

"How's your writing?"

"Good," I answered then look away nervously.

"August, I didn't mean to-,"

"It's okay," I said interrupting him.

I don't want to hear Tommy's name uttered out loud.

"Well, no, it's not. It's just we seemed to be getting close, over those awkward hurtles where we can just be around each other and now, it's-,"

"Weird again," I said.

He nods his head.

I look away, but Miles takes his hand and gently glides my face to face him.

"Weird is okay," he said softly.

Our faces are close, too close again. I can smell his scent, his sweet intoxicating scent.

"Whatever makes you, you. I want to know. I don't care how strange."

I look at his lips, his full kissable lips, at this moment, I want to trace his lips with my tongue. His eyes sparkled like a Jamaican ocean, an aquamarine pool. I slowly inhaled and then slowly pulled away. Chills go through my body again.

"You okay,"

"Chills,"

"Don't fight them," he said. "Let them take over."

# 5

I **WAIT FOR ADAM** to finish reading. Casually I walk around his office looking at the art deco décor of his office. Adam is high maintenance. His office is immaculate, and all of the furniture, desks, chairs, the shelves and rug are all imported from some country. On the walls are pictures of family and friends, certificates as being one of the prominent publishing companies in the state. I notice a couple of large posters standing on easels of new book releases. Upon the walls are posters of his most popular books, one is mine, *The Beautiful Ones.* Also on the wall, he has a few paintings on the wall, there is a bookshelf. I never really looked at his office before. I am usually there to get scolded about why I don't have a book ready or why I don't want to do a book signing. But now as I wait for him, I look at everything as if this is the first time I have been in his office.

As I turned around to look at him, he smiled at me. Adam is so unpredictable. You don't know the message behind his smile. Serial killers have his smile as well as proud fathers. I smile back, waiting for whatever he is about to say or do. As I walk to his desk and sit down in my usual seat, I am nervous about his animated smile.

"This book is amazing," he said "Really amazing,"

As I took a deep breath, I grinned.

"August, within almost three months you have written four books,"

"Novella," I said.

"You say tomato...," he said with a shrug of his shoulders. "We can put them in a collection and call it the August Schofield Project."

"Oooh, something like J.D. Salinger, with Nine Stories," I said with excitement.

"If you start going nuts again looking for your Gatsby, I will kill you," He told me; still smiling.

I chuckle.

"You seemed calm, did you find Gatsby or did you get over your foolish quest,"

I think about my answer. Did I find my Gatsby, my great American novel? While I was in Rome with my friends, I saw the beauty of the city. I saw the Ancient Roman Sights, the Vatican Museums. The Sistine Chapel where Michaelangelo created his Gatsby. I loved the sunrises in Rome, the way the colors blended together to make the dawn almost perfect.

The first few evenings, Miles and I spent those evening in some small village dining on some rich, delicious Italian dish. Miles romanced me, something that no one has ever done. He talked to me about his family, his sister, Lena and their children, about his parents. Like me, Miles had been writing since he was a kid. He fell in love with the book, *To Kill a Mocking Bird*, no specific reason on why he liked the book,

"Atticus Finch, just a smooth cat, ya know," he said to me thinking about the character.

I laughed.

"My girl was Scout," I told him.

"Yeah, she was dangerous,"

"Literature is a powerful method," Miles said. "No one really understands how we or those that study literature fall in love with words. Literature is the art of the written works. Novels, poems, dramas, short stories or novellas, I love them. I love how words come together and just make a story or a song, or something."

I listened to Miles elaborate on his love for words; it was almost comical. He simply loved a good story, be it in a book or song,

"Lyrics to a song," he continued, "people snapping their fingers to the beat, but when they really listen to the lyrics, then the song that they are listening to is another song. Billie Holiday's *Good Morning Heartache*, she said: " 'Good morning heartache, you old gloomy sight, good morning heartache, I thought we said goodbye last night, I tossed and turned until it seemed you had gone-,' "when I finally got to sleep-," but here you are with the dawn,' August, that is some good stuff,"

I was surrounded by greatness, artist whose visions were beyond extraordinary. I looked at Miles who was talking, expressing his love for the arts, from music, to sculptures, to novels. The way his face would light up whenever mentioning someone's work, as if he was a kid in a toy store and the owner allowed him to have one of everything, we both felt the same way about  books; good books, books with souls like Toni Morrison's novels, F. Scott's novels.

"That's why I started *Kirby Howard,* I knew that I could never write the way you do or the way others do, but I can write about why I love the book or why I did not.

I can expound on the contents of the novel or the concepts of the characters,

August, you have a way of capturing a scene. When I read your work, I am right there, in the middle of the accident, an eyewitness, and I see everything. And what I didn't see, I am led or pulled into the direction of searching out whatever it is. I can feel the emotion of the characters. Their intense emotion, their pain or their love, or even their hate. That book, with the couple, I was really feeling my man's pain,"

Then Miles looked at me, I mean really looked at me. His blue eyes pierced through me.

"Since I met you, sometimes I wonder if-," he hesitated,

"What?" I asked.

He chuckled as if he was bashful.

"Tell me," I said with a grin.

"This is going to sound real corny," he said.

I shrugged my shoulders. He took in a deep breath,

"I wonder if you're my classic piece," he said.

"Your classic piece," I asked confused by his statement.

"I was told that *The Count of Monte Cristo,* is the godfather to revenge stories, -there will only be one Edmund Dantes; classic. There will only be one *Pride and Prejudice,* a classic. The independent mind of Elizabeth Bennett was untraditional, but yet she was the kind of woman that I could fall for. You kind of remind me of Mr. Darcy,"

"I remind you of a dude?" I asked laughing.

"No, not a dude," Miles laughed, "But he was somewhat shy and reserved. It made him come off rude, once you got to know he was cool."

"And this is how you saw me?"

"With all due respect August, you do have your stand-offish moments,"

I nodded my head indicating that I was not offended by his comment. I respected what he was saying to me. I know that my weird and something neurotic ways makes me come off snobbish like Mr. Darcy or shy and reserved. But technically I am neither. I get in my anti-social phase and really want to be left alone.

"In spite of your ways," Miles continued. "I get excited whenever I see you because you never know the story with you. You don't see it coming. You maybe stand-offish that can be taken as shy or reserved. Then you are this creative energy that cannot be contained. There is the anxiety and intensity I saw on the plane. You're a writer, a constant current, an unpredictable tide,"

"Wow," I said stunned by his reference.

"You see all this," I said waving my hand at the beauty of my surroundings. "The Sistine Chapel and all the other great works of art that we saw, I want my great piece,"

Miles took in a deep breath,

"You want your Gatsby, this great piece of American Literature so that you too can stand among the great ones, Twain, Faulkner, Salinger,"

"Yes,"

"Why don't you think your work is not standing among them?"

I shrugged my shoulders.

"I don't know,"

"August, I think you are Gatsby," Miles said to me,

"Excuse me,"

"You are looking for the success, not for the American dream, but for the success of the great American novel. After the success of your first book-,"

"Began my quest for Gatsby Greatness," I replied. "I wanted to prove that I am successful."

I suddenly felt foolish.

How did I miss this revelation? As much as I read *The Great Gatsby.* I started writing when I was a kid, at eight years old. I knew that I wanted to be a writer. I wanted to prove that I was worthy of standing with the greats. His lavish parties to get the attention of Daisy was my overactive imagination, my obsession with Tommy. Was he Nick Calloway? I was using him to get to my Daisy, just like Jay was using him to get to her. However, in spite of the secret plot to show off his self –worth. Nick still liked Gatsby. Tommy Gibbs and I never met.

I mused over this revelation. Miles raised his drink as to toast.

"You are a classic- a great American piece," he said to me

"Okay," I said. "Gatsby was cut-throat, a real shark, wouldn't his death somewhat poetic justice,"

"Your person is not entirely Gatsby- just your quest for self-fulfillment, he died alone- He could have had many friends and admirers, but he was cut-throat and pushed people away. August if you're not careful, that can be you."

"I don't mean to be so reclusive or stand-offish, I find a sense of solace when I am alone with my thoughts," I said feeling guilty. "I have no control in my writing, I just go. When it comes to writing, the tide doesn't frighten me, because it's not my life. It is the characters. I just sit back, watch and tell the story."

Miles sipped his wine and then leaned forward to me.

"Let me in," he said softly, "I promise I won't be a disturbance,"

"I know," I said to him. "When I am with you, I am comfortable, strangely comfortable."

"Strangely?"

"I don't have to hide, I mean, with my friends, I have to be available, ready to entertain, but with you- I can just be here,"

He nodded his head.

I looked into his eyes and read them. His blue eyes promised me refuge. I could be me, and he would still care. I could trust him, and all will still be okay. I closed my eyes for a brief moment. I opened them up, and my eyes met his eyes of refuge. There was trust in his eyes, reliance in his eyes.

"Let me settle the check, and we can go for a walk," he said in a soft tone.

It seemed like time stood still just for us. We walked alone. There were others around walked around town, talking among themselves, living their lives- they seemed like insignificant figures. Miles held out his hand to me,

"My hands are clammy," I said feeling almost ashamed.

"It's okay," he assured me.

I put my hand in his, our fingers intertwined and slowly we walked alone. The full moon looked amazingly large, and it seemed close to us. If I put my hand forward, I could probably touch it.

"When's your birthday?" he asked.

"March," I answered. "yours?"

"August-," he said with a grin.

I couldn't help but smile back.

"Coincidence?"

I chuckled lightly,

"No,"

"Why were you named August," he asked.

"Named after August Wilson," I answered. "My father was a big fan of his."

"What about your mom?"

"What was your mom's name?"

"Scarlet," I said smiling. "My father said that she was real fiery hot tempered-but just a ball of fire, energy. My father says that I get my antsy ways from her. Joy looks like my mom, which is why I think Xavier is very overprotective of her."

"My parents wanted my sister and me to sing to be musical prodigies."

"Miles Davis and Lena Horne," I said smiling.

"Yep, and neither of us can hold a note or play a tune," He said.

I laughed.

"What's your favorite color?" he asked.

"I don't have one," I said.

"No," he asked surprised.

"Why are you surprised?" I asks.

He looked me over to inspect me,

"Oh, the black," I laughed, "Um, yeah, I ah, I don't know,"

Miles chuckled. I took a deep breath, not wanting to explain my reason for dressing in all back, I just sighed. Miles smiled at me, indicating that I didn't have to explain. I liked the fact that with him, there was no need to make sense. I can be me.

"You like it," he said.

I nodded.

"Okay,"

"Can I ask you something," I asked.

Miles nodded,

"Something personal,"

"Okay," he said to me,

I waited a moment. His grin indicated he was curious to what was on my mind.

"How come, you don't have children or were you married or-,"

Miles grinned.

"I haven't found the right one to marry, I guess,"

"You guess,"

Miles shrugged almost in a casual way.

"I guess what I am trying to say is, I am not going to fall in love or entertain the concept until I know that she is the woman I love."

I nodded my head accepting his answer. He continued.

"But I know this when you're in love you do things that you usually don't do,"

"Like what?"

"Spontaneous trips across the globe."

I took a deep breath. Afraid to breathe. Did he just say what I think he said? He moved closer towards me, I slowly backed away, but Miles grabbed my arm, holding me. For a moment we looked into each other's eyes, and from the look in his eyes, he said what I thought that he said. Miles was telling me that he loved me, or he thinks that he is in love with me. He nodded his head.

"You don't know me," I said in a whisper. "I could be a psychopath, or some kind of mental case- because I do get goofy sometimes. I could not be the one, you know, the one that could make you happy-,"

Miles took his hands and cupped my face in his palms, one look in his eyes, and I was calm.

"I know you," he said softly, "I know that when I am not around you, I think of you. I know that when you smile, my heart skips a beat. Your antsy demeanor is endearing to me. I can look into your eyes and see that you feel the same, but the wall you have up you won't allow me to come in. It's not fear of commitment, but fear of what I might see. Let down the wall and let me in."

*Tommy.* I thought.

If he knows the truth about Tommy, he may think I am crazy just like everyone else.

"You promise you won't think I'm crazy?" I asked as tears formed into my eyes.

He slowly nodded his head. I slowly took in a deep breath. I moved back away from him to prepare myself to tell him about me and my muse. About the safety that I had in The Land of Aug. How my muse is my only friend. I told him how it started, me seeing him. How it seemed as if Tommy takes me there, into the depth of my creative mind and tells me to: Don't let them see me coming, I don't have a desire to meet him in person. If I do; then I do. If I don't, then I won't, but the creative force that he brings to me is something that is beyond unfathomable. With him, I am in the scene in the middle of it all. I can smell the food cooking. I can smell the season. I can feel the love or hate, I can look into the eyes of my characters, and they look into mine and actually talk to me. Not what I think they would say, but actually talking with me.

"An American classic," Miles said with a grin.

I looked at him wondering what he meant.

"That's the big secret about Tommy Gibbs?"

I nodded my head.

"How do you explain creative hallucinations?" I asked. "You be considered a nut, and you're committed into a nut house."

"But you're a author" he said. "Authors are weird,"

"Thanks,"

"I don't mean it as an insult," he said laughing. "Writers and authors don't fit the norm, or what society says is normal. We do our own thing, write our own story. Live in our own world. Mr. Rogers's had the Land of Make Believe. There was Sesame Street?" he chuckled. "A six-foot bird walking around town, and people talking to him as if that is normal?"

I laughed.

"August, you're not crazy. You're just a creative genius. Now, Gibbs, he is a nut, his work does take you there, so I can see why you do what you do and you produce what you produce, because as mentioned your work is amazing."

Miles and I continued our walk, hand in hand.

"Not everyone sees it that way, they think I need outside activities or psychiatric treatment, and they're writers, they are artistic,"

Miles said. "There is only one August Schofield."

A moment passed before he spoke again.

"Maybe this trip to Rome and be the start of something," Miles said to me.

"I like that," I said. "but what if-,"

"No, no," he said placing his cupping his palm on my face.

I leaned into his hand.

"Don't try to predict the tide, just ride," Miles said.

I slowly moved closer to him and wrapped my arms around his waist. His body felt good in my arms. Miles wrapped his arms around me. I rested my head on his chest and slowly inhaled and then exhaled.

"August," he said softly. "This feels nice,"

I sighed. I felt all the tension and anxiety released from my body. He held me close. I didn't want him to let go.

"Is it okay, that I don't want to let go," I said.

"Yeah,"

I leaned forward and kissed the top of my head.

"I can be here forever if you want."

**"AUGUST," ADAM SAID PULLING** me out of my thoughts.

I smile at him.

"Stop smiling at me," he barks.

He waits for a moment, looking at me trying to read something in me but then looks away.

"Is this Gatsby?" he asks me holding up my manuscript.

"No," I said being vague.

"Okay, you want to be secretive, whatever. This is good work. The vacation did you good. You look like the August I met five years ago, fresh, wide-eyed, ready to share her words."

Adam hands me a folder. I opened it up and see that it was my new contract as well as an advancement check. I quickly read over it and smiled.

"I am sure that you are pleased with the conditions," he said.

I nodded my head. I stand up, "I have to go, but I will be talking with you soon,"

I headed towards the door.

"Aug," he said.

I turned to face him. He holds up my manuscript.

"This is already in production,"

I smile.

"See ya later.

I walk out of the office. Waiting in the front lobby is Joy and X. They look up from their magazines when they see me. I grin. Together they stand up. I put my hand out towards Joy. She quickly runs towards me and takes my hand into hers. And within moments we're outside. I see Tommy standing across the street. For a moment I stood still staring at him. Then I look down at my Joy, she looks up at me with her big brown eyes and smiles. I look at my brother, and he is smiling at me. I take a deep breath, and together we walk down the street for some ice cream, leaving Tommy behind.